FINDING HOME

FINDING HOME

KRISTIE LEIGH

EDITED BY
WALLFLOWER EDITS

COVER DESIGN BY
VANILLA LILY DESIGNS

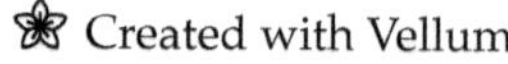 Created with Vellum

2020 hasn't been the greatest year for us all—to say the least
—so I hope that "Finding Home" brings a smile to your face.

Merry Christmas

&

Happy New Year

ONE

CHARLOTTE

"IT'S everything I ever dreamed it would be Dylan." I was in awe the moment we stepped into the lobby of Hale Court Inn. My sundress billowed in the wind from the cross breeze through the open foyer. "This is going to be the best Christmas ever."

His arm wrapped around my shoulder. "It's decent. I'm sure we will have a great time."

Dylan had grown up privileged so he had no idea what this felt like for me. I'd barely left New York my entire life. I'd never even been on a plane before.

"It's exactly like it looked in the magazines." Most things are dressed up for advertising so I was shocked it wasn't.

We slowly approached the front desk where a petite blond named Mindy greeted us. "Welcome to Hale Court Inn. Can I get your name please?" Her smile was bright and genuine as she made eye contact with Dylan.

I wandered off to look around while he checked us in. The lobby was open to the outdoors allowing the sea air to blow through. I stood at the back balcony overlooking the ocean and breathed it all in. My eyes stung with unshed tears. I couldn't believe after three years of scrimping and saving I was finally here.

I remember the day I was flipping through a magazine and came across the most adorable yet extravagant boutique inn. I fell in love and vowed to start saving. Although my research of pricing had my heart stopping it hadn't deterred me. I told myself that one day was better than never in my books because the wait would make it all the more worth it.

When Dylan and I first started dated a year and a half ago I told him all about it. He immediately offered to take me. I knew that he could more than afford to pay but I really wanted to do it on my own. I had been saving for over a year already at that point so I declined his offer.

Strong arms wrapped around me from behind. "Got the keys babe. Are you ready to christen the room?" Leave it to Dylan that his first thoughts are about having sex.

I sighed. "We have plenty of time for that. I don't want to waste our vacation in bed. We could do that at home for free. Plus we have to go to bed at night can't you wait until then?" I wasn't in the habit of turning him down. Dylan was a man after all and sex was a priority on most days but I paid a lot of money for this and I wanted to enjoy every minute of it.

He let out a heavy groan as he pushed back from the railing. "You're such a prude."

I was honestly far from a prude and he was well aware of that but he transformed into a big man baby whenever he was turned down—which wasn't often.

My stomach rumbled alerting me to the fact that it was way past dinner time for me. I turned to face him and plastered on a smile. "Why don't we grab something to eat and then we could go for a romantic walk on the beach?"

"Whatever you want to do Charlotte." He could be such a condescending asshole sometimes but I wasn't going to let his mood ruin things for me. This was my dream vacation and I was going to enjoy every minute of it.

I smiled and waved at Mindy as we walked by but she wasn't paying me much attention.

My stomach knotted as the row of bungalows came into view. Each one was a different color from pink to aqua to green to yellow. They all had their own wrap around porch and a second story.

Dylan stopped in front of a yellow one. "This is us."

He turned to me and kissed my cheek. It seemed his cranky attitude had shifted.

Thank God because I had very specific ideas on how this trip would go so I was glad to see he was coming around.

We walked up the steps and he opened the door for me. I stepped inside to find the entire suite was floor to ceiling windows and had an adorable winding staircase that I assume would lead to the bedroom upstairs.

I was speechless as I walked around. It was exactly as I'd visualized it would be.

Dylan stood by the staircase and cleared his throat. "There's still time to head to the bedroom before we eat."

I let Dylan's words go in one ear and out the other as I opened the back sliders and stepped out onto the porch. We had an unobstructed view of the ocean in front of us. It was breathtaking.

A tear slipped down my cheek but I brushed it away. It was a happy tear. I knew Dylan didn't understand because he'd spent his entire life with money and probably went to places like this all the time but for me this was more like a once in a lifetime opportunity. I worked hard to pay for this trip and it felt extremely rewarding to be here—finally.

"I found the room service menu, they close in less

than an hour." He handed the binder to me and leaned against the railing with his back to the water.

My brow furrowed. "I can't believe you're so indifferent to such beauty."

He shrugged. "It's just the ocean."

It was kind of sad to watch someone be so spoiled that they took everything for granted. I quickly picked something my meal and handed it back to him so he could go order for us. I wasn't going to waste time with dinner when I could be enjoying the magnificence before me. I wasn't sure why Dylan was being such a douche canoe because he truly was a nice guy most of the time. Something seemed to be bothering him but for now I wasn't going to worry about it. I kicked off my flip flops and stepped down from the porch. The sand felt like heaven between my toes as I walked toward the shoreline.

I'd always loved the ocean and enjoyed our warmer summer months but our beaches were nothing like this. Winter and snow were not for me. New York had always been my home but stepping out onto this beach had me feeling like I was destined for somewhere hot and definitely by a beach.

The water was refreshing as it splashed up against my legs when I reached the surf. I couldn't resist the urge and I dove in sundress and all. The water was fairly calm with only small waves so I laid back and floated on my back as I looked up at the darkening sky. I still couldn't believe this was going to be my life for the next two weeks. I felt like I was truly blessed.

"Charlotte!" Dylan's voice broke me out of my haze and I stood up in the water. He was laughing at me. "You're a lunatic. You know there's such a thing as a bathing suit right?"

I rolled my eyes. "Of course I do but I couldn't help myself."

He shook his head but still had a smirk on his face. "Well come on and get dried off. Dinner is here."

After getting changed into some night shorts and a tank I walked out back to find Dylan had set up the table with a lantern for us to eat. "Your dinner awaits." He gestured to the seat as he pulled it out.

I approached and kissed him on the cheek before taking my seat. "Thank you. This is so sweet of you."

He sat down across from me and sighed. "Sorry I've been in a mood. I just have a lot going on."

I reached over the table and took his hand in mine. "It's okay. Let's try and forget about real life for the next two weeks and enjoy this much needed time away."

He smiled in return and lifted the domes from our food. The aroma that wafted from them was to die for. My mouth was watering instantly and I couldn't wait to dig into the steak and veggies I had before me.

We enjoyed our meal and Dylan's mood seemed to perk up a little. We took that walk along the beach I'd wanted and held hands as we talked about nothing important. He was a workaholic and almost always talked about work but he kept most of the conversation away from his job which I was exceptionally grateful for. Dylan didn't purposely make me feel like I was beneath him but when he talked about his job and all the important things he did as an investment banker it made me feel like my job at the bar I managed was irrelevant. Okay I know it wasn't a *significant* career choice but I loved my job and although it didn't afford me the luxuries that his job did I wouldn't trade it for anything. Well maybe for living here because I was sure I could find a bar down here to manage and look out over the water all day.

What a hard gig that would be.

I chuckled to myself as I foolishly let my mind go to places it never had.

"What are you giggling about?" Dylan looked down at me.

"Nothing much." I squeezed his hand lightly. "Could you imagine living in a beautiful paradise like this? Waking up to this every morning?"

He shook his head. "Not at all. I love the hustle and pace of the city. There's nothing that would ever entice me enough to leave that behind. Don't be ridiculous."

"I could picture it." But could I do it? Move to the beach? I shook it off. My whole life was back in the states and I couldn't just up and move.

The island air was doing strange things to me. I needed to get some sleep

I couldn't wait to see what the morning looked like on Malgaho Island.

———

THE SUN SHINED bright through the open doors and the sheer curtains swayed back and forth in the wind. I smiled as my brain caught up with where I was. Rolling over I found Dylan's side of the bed was empty but there was a note on his pillow. *Gone to the gym. Breakfast when I get back.*

As much as I hated the gym I wanted to spend this vacation with him and he loved to work out so I reluctantly threw on a pair of leggings and a sports bra.

I sighed as I looked out the window. The ocean tugged at my heart but I headed toward the torture room they called a gym instead. The double glass doors were heavy as I opened them and stepped into the cool air of the facilities which I found empty. I walked around the corner to see if maybe Dylan was in the changerooms or sauna but he was nowhere to be found.

I smiled to myself. I bet he'd taken a different route back to the house and grabbed us breakfast on the way back to surprise me in bed.

I gripped the handle of the door but paused when I heard what sounded like Dylan's voice. I stayed quiet trying to hear which direction it came from.

"Put your leg right there. That's it." His gruff voice came from behind a door in the corner of the room. I must've missed another part of the gym. He was always so helpful with others when he was working out.

I smiled knowing he'd be surprised that I was coming to join him for his workout and opened the door.

His ass faced me as he pounded into Mindy the front desk clerk from behind. He was surprised all right but not for the same reason I'd expected. Although he was looking at me he didn't bother stopping his pounding rhythm. Mindy turned her head and immediately tried to pull away from Dylan but his hand held her in place at the nape of her neck. I let go of the door and let it close without so much as a word. My feet carried me backward slowly.

"Ward can't find out about this. Oh. My. God." Mindy let out a moan. "Seriously. Holy shit. Ohhhh. I'll lose my job and him." Mindy didn't seem too concerned as her whimpers of pleasure continued to fill the room.

I finally broke out of my trance and ripped open the gym doors and bolted for the suite.

I walked through the door and went straight upstairs. Thank God I hadn't got around to unpacking anything so there were only a few things to gather before heading back out and to the lobby.

There was another blond girl at the front desk. She must have noticed my demeaner because her first question was if I was okay.

I took a deep breath. "Is there anywhere available for me to stay?" I tried not to cry but the damn tears started. I was more angry than sad at this point.

How the fuck could he?

She typed away on her computer and then looked up at me with a sad smile. "I'm sorry miss we don't have anything available. Was your room not to your satisfaction? I'd love to try and help in any way possible to make things right."

"I don't think you can do anything to help this situation. I need my *own* bed without my boyfriend—well ex-boyfriend now."

She smiled again. "I'm sure there is something we can do to help. I can get the—"

Someone cleared their throat and I looked up to find chocolate brown eyes gazing back at me.

"How can I help you?" His Adam's apple bobbed as he spoke and his accent had me holding my legs together. I wasn't sure what kind of accent it was but it almost sounded English.

I stared at him willing my voice to come but I couldn't do anything but gawk. He was sexy. His hair was short and spiked on the top of his head and he had the perfect amount of scruff. I could see a hint of a tattoo poking out on his forearm under his rolled up sleeve of his dress shirt.

I swallowed hard and snapped myself out of it.

TWO
WARD

SHE HADN'T SAID A WORD. If I hadn't known better I would've thought she was deaf.

I walked out of my office knowing I'd regret this but ultimately it was my job to make each guest happy. I stepped around the counter to stand in front of the destressed woman. "My name is Ward. Let me know what I can do for you."

She just shook her head and laughed as she looked up at the ceiling. "Karma was working its ways already." Her smile had a wicked edge to it. "Ward is it?"

"Yup! Ward Hale at your service. My parents had a thing for weird names." I shrugged. I knew it was an unusual name and I had been teased all my youth for it but as I got older I'd been told by many women it sounded powerful and strong.

She nodded before looking toward Tammy behind the desk and then back to me. "Can we speak in private?"

"Of course. Let's talk in my office." I took her luggage and led the way shutting the door behind us. "Have a seat." I pointed to the chair and then took a seat at my desk. "I'm sorry I didn't get your name."

She took a few deep breaths "My name is Charlotte. Do you know someone named Mindy? Blond bimbo that works at your front desk."

Damn it! I cleared my throat and held back a smile. "Umm yes I do."

"Well I just caught her bent over in the storage closet of the gym being railed by my *ex*-boyfriend." Her smile looked smug.

Was she taking pleasure in telling me that my girlfriend was cheating on me? I guess the saying goes misery loves company.

I dropped my head and scrubbed my hands down my face. "Fucking Mindy." I wasn't going to get into my relationship issues with this woman. I knew Mindy was quite promiscuous but I thought we'd discussed being exclusive once we started living together. Clearly she hadn't received that memo.

I turned my attention to the problem at hand. She needed somewhere to stay and since this problem was caused by not only my girlfriend but she just happened to be an employee I needed to make this right. "I'm so sorry ma'am that is definitely not what I wanted to hear. I know we don't have any rooms available and you don't know me from Adam but you could stay with me. It seems that I'll have the space now since *someone* won't be living with me anymore and it's the least I could do."

Her eyes went wide but she quickly recovered. "Honestly right now I would stay anywhere as long as it was away from *him*. I'll call my parents once they are off work and see if they can get me a flight home. I literally spent every penny I have on this trip."

I felt horrible. I knew the cost of coming here to the inn wasn't cheap and I didn't want anyone to leave with a sour taste in their mouth. I stood and came back around to stand in front of her. I leaned back against the desks edge and crossed my outstretched legs attempting to seem casual. "Have you ever been to the island before?"

She shook her head. "No. I've been saving for three years for this trip and in less than twenty-four hours he has completely ruined it for me."

Fucking asshole. I'd never understood why people cheated. If you weren't happy why didn't you just leave?

"Please don't let him ruin it for you. I know your vacation started off on the wrong foot but don't let him win. You've earned this vacation and you deserve it—especially now." I crouched down in front of her to look her in the eyes. "Listen, I don't spend a lot of time at home. I'm kind of a workaholic, hence why I live on the property. You're welcome to stay as long as you'd like. Please enjoy the island and all it has to offer. I'll even show you around."

"Didn't you just say you were a workaholic?"

She was right. I wouldn't have much time but maybe I could make time. "We will figure something out."

"You really don't have to do that. Offering up somewhere to stay so I can try and make something of this vacation is more than I could've dreamed."

I let Tammy know I'd be out for the rest of the day but I'd have my radio if she needed me. Sam would be in shortly and he was plenty capable of handling anything that came our way.

"Are you sleeping with her too?" Charlotte asked as we headed out the side door to where my bungalow was. "Don't answer that. It's none of my business."

I stopped in my tracks. "No. It's definitely not any of your business but the answer is no. I don't make it a point to sleep with my employees. I was in a committed relationship with Mindy—or so I'd thought."

I looked Charlotte up and down appraisingly. She

wasn't my type in any way. She was brunette and had that girl next door look going on. I was usually into the blond *bimbo* type as Charlotte so eloquently put it. Her body was hot though and her outfit left nothing to the imagination.

She was blushing by the time my eyes came back up to meet hers. "Fair enough. I lived with Dylan too. Ugh! Guess I'm also homeless." She smiled up at me and batted her long lashes dramatically. "How long did you say I could stay for?"

I just shook my head. This girl was going to be trouble but if I was being honest I could use the distraction and it would force me to take a little step back from work like I'd been meaning to anyway.

When we got to my place I slipped the key card into the slot and opened the door allowing Charlotte to enter first. She walked in and set her purse down on the ottoman and I put her luggage to the side of the door.

"Wow. This place is stunning. I thought our place was amazing but this...this is mind-blowing." She walked to the back doors and looked out over the ocean. "There's something about this place that calms me." She turned back to face me. "My life is literally in shambles right now. I should be having a complete mental breakdown but somehow I'm doing okay."

I sat down at the bar and smiled. "You're on

Malgaho Island. This is no place for a meltdown. Save it for when you get home."

"Sounds like a plan to me. I'll bottle everything up and enjoy the holidays on this beautiful piece of heaven you call home."

I grabbed two glasses and a bottle of whiskey and held it up. "Drink?"

Her brow furrowed as she looked at the bottle. "It's not even lunch time."

I shrugged and poured us each a glass. "We're on island time. From the famous words of Jimmy Buffet himself it's five o'clock somewhere."

"I think we could actually be friends."

I handed her the drink and we clinked glasses. "Cheers to that. I'm glad you think so since we're going to be living together for a couple weeks."

"True that."

We finished our drinks and I showed her to the guest room. Unfortunately for her the view from that room wasn't as good as the master but she didn't seem at all put out by that.

"I appreciate this more than you'll ever know." She reached up and wrapped her arms around me catching me off guard.

After a second I snapped out of it and hugged her back. "You're very welcome. I think we are going to have an awesome time and you're going to head home thinking this was the best vacation ever."

She stepped back and smiled. "I think so too and I believe we should start with another whiskey while we order lunch."

"Sounds like a plan." I knew she didn't have much as far as funds went so ordering room service was my way of treating her and chalking it up to a perk of the job. I highly doubt she picked up on the connection between my last name and the resort so I was hoping to keep it that way. People always treated me differently when they found out who I was.

We went back downstairs and grabbed the menu and we both decided on burgers and fries. I had the chef add the sauce I loved so much and told them we'd be out back.

"Do you eat room service for every meal? I don't think I'd ever cook again if I worked here."

We sat down on the loungers on the back porch. "I used to but I'm kind of over it. When we do a revamp of the menu I order for a while and then it gets old."

She nodded and curled her legs up under her. "Yeah I could see that. Does this view ever get old?" She put her hand up before I could answer. "Don't answer that. I want to go home thinking that it gets boring when I'm holed up in New York freezing my ass off."

"Yeah probably better I don't answer that one."

She smacked me on the arm playfully.

"You know I've never seen snow? When I was a kid we went to Tennessee once for Christmas with promises of snow but it never did. Not one flake. It was cold as hell though."

Her shoulder shook with laughter. "I bet you island folk can't handle the cold. If I'm being honest I'm not a fan myself but I do love how pretty snow looks on Christmas morning."

"I'd love to have a white Christmas at least once in my lifetime. Maybe Alaska is the best option to ensure snow."

Room service interrupted our conversation. We ate in mostly comfortable silence and finished of our whiskey.

"Do you want to take a walk? I feel like after eating that massive burger we should burn a few calories." She got up and waited for my response.

I really should say no and go back to work—that's what I'd generally do but instead I stood and said, "Why not?"

She started off toward the south but I grabbed her arm. "I'd suggest we head the opposite direction if you want to avoid your boyfriend and Mindy."

She pointed at me and winked. "Now that's a great idea. I'm definitely not ready to face that head on. The visions of them..." She pushed against my shoulder. "You know he didn't even stop? He just looked at me and continued fucking her like I meant absolutely nothing to him."

I wasn't sure how to respond. My instincts told me to find this guy and beat the ever loving shit out of him. Who cheated on their girlfriend? On vacation no less. I held back the unfathomable anger I was feeling and decided to speak instead. "Some men are complete pigs...well some women are too." It wasn't very deep but I really didn't want to talk about Mindy if I was being truthful.

She sighed. "We'd been together a year and a half. How long had you and Mindy been together?"

I guess we were going there. "We've been together almost two years. Our anniversary is coming up and we're going away for a week."

She blinked a few times as she stared back at me. "You mean you're *still* going?"

"Things with Mindy are forever *complicated*. She's always been...free spirited I guess you could say. She's trying."

She chuckled. "I'm sorry." She gestured toward me. "You're a reasonably good-looking guy—if you like the big burly sexy type—why would you put up with that? You deserve better."

I ignored the word *reasonably* and responded. "Not

that I owe you an explanation but our arrangement works for us. I am a complete workaholic and that seems to be an issue for every other woman I've tried dating. Before we moved in together we weren't *exclusive* but I did think we were after. Don't get me wrong I won't be taking this lightly. I'll be making her squirm but I guess what I'm trying to say is I'd rather have Mindy than be alone."

"I'm sorry."

I shook my head. I didn't want pity. It worked for me.

"No. I'm sorry you feel that you need to settle. There are women out there that can accept a workaholic but there's also a woman out there that's so perfect for you that you'd blow off work just to spend the day watching movies with her." She smiled sadly.

I definitely didn't want her feeling sorry for me. That wasn't what I was going for.

I looked over and saw her swipe a tear from her cheek. "I'm such an idiot."

I stopped walking and turned to her. "What? Why would you say that?"

"I just spoke those words out loud and realized that although I adjusted my work schedule for Dylan I wasn't important enough for him to ever blow off work for. I guess I never comprehended that before now. I was settling with him and I never wanted that for myself. I deserve someone that would cross the earth for me and Dylan wasn't that guy."

I was never really good at talking about feelings. The urge to scoop her up and hold her close was overwhelming but it would also completely inappropriate. "Sometimes we don't see what's staring us right in the face. It's one of the flaws us humans have unfortunately."

"You're telling me."

THREE

CHARLOTTE

MORNING WAS NOT my favorite part of the day. I worked in a bar so I slept in most mornings after being out late. My favorite time of day was when I walked out of the bar in the wee hours of the morning. When things were quiet and there was no one else around.

I stumbled out of the bathroom stubbed my toe on the door jamb. "Ow shit."

"Are you okay?" Ward's deep voice came from down the hall.

"Yeah sorry." I peeked around his door jamb. "Did I wake you?"

He shook his head. "No I've been up for a while. I always wake at the same time every day well unless I'm already at work of course. Six sharp."

I lifted my wrist and looked at my watch. "Six huh?"

"Every morning." He looked so proud of himself.

I hummed with a smirk on my face. "What time do you have to be at work?"

"I actually don't have a set schedule."

I held in my chuckle and kept my face stoic. "Good thing."

His brow furrowed. "Why is that?"

"Because it's nearly nine."

He jumped out of bed and strode toward me and grabbed my wrist inspecting the watch. "This is New York time right? You're just messing with me." His laugh was awkward.

"It's no big deal. People sleep in sometimes and if you aren't actually *late* for work. What's the harm?" I wasn't sure why he was acting so off. Had he really never slept in before?

He stepped back and started to pace. "I've *never* in my adult life slept in. Not *once*."

"Not even after a drunken night or late night sexcapades?" I was kind of shocked. I slept in every single chance I got.

He stopped pacing and leaned forward placing his hands on either side of me on the door jamb. "Never." He shook his head incredulously. "Do you have some sort of voodoo magic you played on me?"

I burst out laughing. "You caught me. I'm a witch

and my sole mission in life is to make men fall into such a deep spell that they sleep in for a few hours."

"Ugh!" He pushed back off the moulding. "I'm going to shower and then order brunch. You game?"

"For the shower or brunch? Or both?" I winked and he just rolled his eyes and shook his head.

He was really fun to mess with. He needed to lighten up a little and that just became my single purpose for being here. I was going to bring the fun back out of Ward. I was sure that deep down he wasn't always a stick in the mud adult.

Ward popped around the corner with his towel around his waist. "Shower's all yours."

I stared at him without responding. I couldn't speak. It seemed that Mr. Fuddy-Duddy was hiding some major abs under those clothes. And that vee…I drew in a sharp breath. My eyes roamed across his chest and down his arm where that tattoo covered his arm completely. It was a beautiful design that I couldn't stop looking at.

"Earth to Charlotte." Ward snapped his fingers in front of my face. "Are you okay?"

I swallowed hard and tried to breathe which was difficult with that chest so close to me now. His scent wafting toward me. "Yeah yeah. Sorry. Shower." I felt like such an idiot. I needed some breathing room. I'd never in my life lost braincells because of abs—although I'd never seen abs like *that* in real life.

Get your shit together girl.

He chuckled. "Can I order us breakfast or do you want me to wait?"

"I'm good with anything as long as there is a lot of coffee with heavy cream and sugar I'll be a happy girl." I threw the covers off me and hopped out of bed.

Ward cleared his throat. I looked back at him to find his eye raking down my body.

I bent over a little more digging into my suitcase. "Are there towels in the bathroom?" I was confident in my skin and although I was wearing a thin tank and panties right now I knew I looked good.

He nodded.

"Great. I'll meet you downstairs. I'll be quick." I strutted passed him with a little extra pep in my step. I took the quickest shower known to womankind. Thank God I got waxed from head to toe before this trip so I didn't have to worry about that.

I threw on a bikini before covering up with a pair of cut off jean shorts and a worn tee and tossed my hair in a messy bun.

I slowly rounded the corner just in case he was shirtless again so I could prepare myself. Thankfully he was fully clothed but instead of his stuffy work clothes he had on a t-shirt and board shorts with flip flops. The casual look worked for him surprisingly.

The smell of coffee had me picking up my pace to the back porch where he was standing. "What's with the get-up? Not going to work?"

"I need to stop by the front desk and have them reprogram my key code and get you a card but other than that I thought we could just hang out."

My jaw must've hit the floor. "Mister workaholic himself is blowing off work? I don't even know you and I feel like that's a *huge* milestone for you. Like *huge.*"

"Shut up and make your coffee." He handed me a mug and leaned against the railing with his own cup.

I wasn't one to ever turn down coffee so I went to work making it and sat down on his porch swing. "I could really get used to this."

"Is all your family in New York?"

I nodded. "Yeah my parents. What about you? You have family nearby?"

He sat down at the table and loaded up his plate. "Everyone lives on the island. Mom, dad, brother and sister as well as her husband and daughter."

"That must be nice. I wish. I always wanted siblings." I downed the last of my cup of coffee before making myself a plate and sitting opposite him.

"Maybe you'll marry into a large family. I think I

like my brother-in-law better than my real brother most days."

He was right. I really did like spending time with Dylan's sister. Probably more than I liked him if I was being honest. The more I thought about it the more I realized that Dylan was never the one for me.

A change of subject was in order. "Do you have big plans for Christmas? Do you guys decorate a palm tree?"

"You city folk…" He shook his head. "No, we use a fake tree because my mom's allergic. And yes we have breakfast as a family on Christmas day, open stockings after that and spend the day just hanging out until dinner. We open presents after dinner."

I sighed. "That sounds nice. We just have dinner and open gifts and then I head home. My family isn't big on holidays so it's never a big affair. This year I'll hang on the beach and drink. I was kind of looking forward to it. I will FaceTime my parents and say Merry Christmas but then I'd go back to drinking and suntanning. It'll be Instagram worthy."

"A relaxing Christmas sounds nice."

I smiled and finished up my breakfast.

"I'm going to head to the get the locks changed and I'll be back shortly."

I curled up in the swing again with my second cup

of coffee. "I'll be right here enjoying my coffee and this amazing view."

After coffee number three my bladder was about to explode and the water was calling my name. After the bathroom I stripped out of my clothes and grabbed a towel and headed back downstairs.

"You've got to be shittin' me." A woman's voice could be heard on the other side of the front door. The door handle jiggled. "What the fuck Ward?" She shouted.

I stood there snickering realizing that Ward had the right idea to change the lock code and that must be Mindy who sounded pissed and I couldn't' be happier.

The sound of a knock on the door caused me to jump back slightly. *Do I answer?* I debated for a moment and then said screw it. I dropped my towel, straightened my bikini and squared my shoulders before opening the door with confidence.

Mindy's face was priceless. Her jaw tightened and her eyes narrowed.

"Can I help you?" I leaned against the door frame casually like I owned the place.

She scowled. "Move aside. I live here."

"I'm sorry sweetie but I'm not able to let you in. If you lived here you would have a *working* key card." My eyes flicked down to her hand. "And since you don't I think you need to scurry back to whatever hole you crawled out of." I shooed her off but she didn't flinch.

She made a noise in her throat that almost sounded like a low growl. "Ward won't ever leave me. He'll come crawling back." She sounded so confident. She smirked and turned with a hair flip out of a teen movie and stormed off.

"Good luck with that." I called after her before slamming the door.

My stomach clenched at the thought of Ward crawling back to her. I didn't know him at all but anyone deserved better than that. She knew she had him by the balls and I couldn't understand why. He had so much going for him and yet he played in the trenches with that hussy? I needed to help him see he was worthy of so much more than that.

I wasn't going to let her ruin my day. Instead I picked up my towel and headed out back to lay in the sun. My fair skin needed a little color.

I set the alarm on my phone for thirty minutes so I didn't burn and laid down on my stomach.

My phone rang just as the alarm went off. Dylan's face popped up on the screen. My heart hammered in my chest. No way was I going to talk to him. I hit ignore and put it back down. I stared at it willing it to disappear along with all the problems in my life. No such luck. It chimed with a text.

Dylan: You're staying with her boyfriend? Wow! That's low!

Is he seriously questioning my morals right now?

Me: I'm sorry my boyfriend FUCKED someone else WHILE I WATCHED and left me essentially HOMELESS in a FOREIGN COUNTRY!

I was shaking I was so mad. "How dare he?"

"How dare who?" Ward blocked the sun as he came to stand in front of me.

I let out of a heavy sigh. "Dylan." I held up my phone. "Your girlfriend popped by earlier and she was none too impressed when her key card didn't work and got a little pissed when I refused to let her in. I guess she ran back to Dylan and told him I was here."

My phone went off again.

Ward snatched the phone from my hand before I could look at it. "Don't answer it. Just delete it. It's none of his business where you are and you deserve better."

I stood and tried to grab the phone but he had a good eight inches on me. "That's rich coming from you. Mindy even said you'd never leave her and you'll come crawling back. At least I have the dignity to tell him off and I will never take him back.

Cheating is one hundred percent a deal breaker." I tried to grab the phone again. "Jesus. Dylan literally had his dick in your girlfriend and you seem to not give a shit."

He pushed my phone at me and stormed off inside the house. Guess I'd struck a nerve with that last bit.

Dylan: I never left you without somewhere to stay. You're welcome back in our cottage any time. Baby what are you doing with him? I'm where you belong.

I cringed as I heard his voice calling me baby. What was wrong with him?

Me: Like fuck. I don't ever want to see you again.

As much as I hated to admit it. Ward was right. I needed to delete and ignore. This was toxic. I quickly blocked his number and deleted the conversation before another text could come through.

"Men!" I wanted punch something.

My heart was racing and I felt like I was having a panic attack. I needed to calm down. Why did I let him get to me like that?

I knew I needed to talk to Ward but I also needed to calm myself before I did that. I was upset with him for getting involved but I was way out of line with how I reacted to him.

Going for a swim would help cool me off in more ways than one so I headed for the ocean and dove in. The water was perfect and exactly what I needed. I waded through the surf trying to clear my mind of all things Dylan. If he hadn't cheated I would've thought he was jealous from the tone of his texts. But I knew better. He was being possessive and that's it. The old saying that *you only want what you can't have* definitely rang true.

"How dare he?" I shook my head. No. No more thoughts of him. I took some deep breaths as I let the waves carry me.

I felt something brush against my leg and I opened my eyes to find Ward standing before me. "I'm sorry. I never should have—"

I waved him off. "I'm sorry. What I said was completely uncalled for. Your relationship is none of my business and I shouldn't have pushed you. You were right and I should've never answered him in the first place. I blocked him."

"Good but I still apologize as well even though I was right." He smirked. "I already explained to you that Mindy and I have an arrangement that works."

I shook my head. "You keep calling it an arrangement? Like what about a *relationship*?"

"Arrangement is a better word for what we have. I don't feel for her like that. I enjoy the times we are together but when we're apart I'm indifferent. The one thing you are right about is her sleeping around. That's not going to be tolerated and I'll be making that clear *if* our arrangement is to continue." He let out a breath. "I feel better. Do you feel better?"

"Yes. Now that we've cleared the air—" I didn't get another word out before he picked me up and threw me what felt like a hundred yards before I splashed into the water again."

I broke up through the surface laughing. "What the hell Ward?"

"It's all part of swimming right?"

I splashed his face but my tiny hands didn't move the water as much as his did. The massive amount he splashed at me went in every orifice of my face. "Fuck."

We spent the next couple hours swimming and talking. It was exactly what I needed. By the time we exited the water I was starving and my eyes were stinging from the saltwater but it was worth it because we'd had a great time letting go and being in the moment. It felt good to not worry about anything but that instant and nothing more.

My stomach growled. "Do you think there's somewhere we could go and eat and not run into

Mindy or Dylan?" I hated to bring them up again but I was hoping to get out and not worry about running into them.

Ward ran his towel down his body and I followed it's every move. Those abs were honestly hypnotic. I'd only ever seen a body like his on the front of romance covers and I'd always thought they were photoshopped. He dropped the towel on the back of a chair. "I think I know a place."

I threw my shorts and tee back on and we headed out to a place called *The Filthy Marlin*. I had to admit the name fit. I would've never expected Ward to step foot in a place that looked like this but everyone seemed to know him by name.

"Come here often?"

He shrugged. "A little. Mindy isn't a fan so it's one of my faves."

I cocked a brow.

"Don't read into it." He handed me a menu. "I know it doesn't look like it but every single item on that piece of paper is to die for. I've been trying to get Marlin to come work for us for years but no such luck."

A man came out from the back who looked to be in his mid-sixties. "Hell no. I'll die in this place." He looked between the two of us. "Finally switched it up and got rid of the bimbo huh?"

I couldn't stop the snort that escaped my nose.

"Shut it old man." He gestured toward me. "Marlin this is Charlotte. Charlotte this is the owner of this fine establishment Marlin."

He reached out his hand and I took it. "Nice to meet you." He pointed at my shirt with the pen. *Drinks by Design*? White Plains, New York right?"

I looked down at my tee. "Yup you been?"

He nodded. "Yeah." He looked up in contemplation. "Probably twenty years ago now. The concept of that place was pretty cool."

"It really is. I've worked there since I could serve."

He raised a brow. "What's that been two years? You look like a baby."

"Seven. I'm twenty-five." I set down my menu. "So I hear everything's good here so why don't you surprise me?"

He slapped Ward on the shoulder. "She's a young one. She'll keep you on your toes." Smiling he picked the menus up off the table. "A surprise it is. Do I get to try and amaze you with my drink making skills too?"

"Sure. Have at it as long as it's not peach I'll drink it."

He walked back behind the bar and punched in our orders and started making our drinks.

I was curious now so I had to ask. "How old are you?"

His brow shot up. "Isn't that a rude question?"

"Only if you ask a woman." I shrugged.

"Thirty-two."

I just nodded. From looking at him I would've pegged him for late twenties but from talking to him I would've late thirties because he was a little stuffy most times but maybe that was just how serious his life was with work.

"So what's so cool about *Drinks by Design*?" He nodded to my tee.

I shrugged. "Basically it's a regular bar but there are some stations set up for groups that allow you to *design* whatever drinks you want. It's really popular for showers or bachelorettes that kind of thing. It's pretty cool I guess and sometimes we feature the drinks that are really good on a special menu and name it after the designer."

"Sounds like an interesting concept. Maybe I'll stop by when I come in search of my white Christmas."

I smiled. "Sounds like a plan. I'll be there."

Marlin came back with our drinks. "Hope you like it." He didn't wait around for me to try it.

I took a sip and it was really good. "This is awesome! I'm actually shocked because I can't put my finger on the ingredients. Usually I can pick them apart." I lifted my glass to Marlin who was standing behind the bar. "I'm impressed."

He nodded with a faint smile on his lips.

"I think we should go dancing."

Ward coughed as he choked on his drink. "Pardon me?"

"I think we should go dancing. Is that a problem?"

He shook his head. "Nope." His throat bobbed as he swallowed hard. "I will go *with* you but I don't dance."

That actually surprised me. He looked like he could bust a move or two. "At all?"

"Nope but I know a place that has a great DJ on Thursday nights. I can watch and enjoy the music while you shake it on the dance floor."

I sighed and took another sip of my drink. "I guess I could wait two days but today we're going to have lots to drink and have fun. Right?"

"I think I can handle that but not sure you can keep up with me in the drinking department."

I couldn't help but laugh. "You're talking to a career bartender. I may weigh half of what you do but I can assure you I can keep up. You spend ninety percent of your days behind a desk and I highly doubt you get out and party. Maybe you have a whiskey or two to help you sleep at night." I cocked a brow. "Tell me I'm wrong."

"We will see."

I knew I was right and I would prove it tonight.

————

"HOW YOU FEELING THERE BIG GUY?" I stood in Ward's bedroom door with my coffee in hand. I was feeling amazing because I made sure to drink two glasses of water and take Advil before bed. Ward on the other hand said he didn't need it.

He groaned and threw the covers over his head. "Why are you so chipper this morning? And if that's coffee I smell you better have one ready for me since you woke me up."

"Well aren't we full of joy this morning. I'll go make you a cup and I promise not to say *I told you so* until after you've drank at least half of it. I'll meet you downstairs." I turned on my heel and walked away before he could say anything.

A few minutes later Ward walked—more like stomped—down the stairs.

"Good morning princess." I handed him his mug. "We should sit outside, the salt air will do you some good but you might want to bring your sunglasses. I'm sure you won't be a fan of the bright sun right now."

He shook his head but grabbed them off the counter. "What time is it?"

"Ten."

He spit out the sip of coffee he'd just taken. "Holy shit! What are you doing to me?"

"Hey, I'm only here for so long. You'll go back to your boring life when I'm gone but for now I'm liking the freer version of Ward."

He sipped his coffee without responding.

"Were you always this uptight?"

I couldn't see his eyes but if the way his forehead was wrinkling was any indication he was glaring something fierce at me. "I'm not *uptight*. I just have responsibilities here.

"Most adults have responsibilities but doesn't it feel good to let loose every once and a while?"

He set his coffee mug down and turned to face me. "As much as I hate to admit it. You're right. It really does. I truly haven't had fun in so long."

"Yay! I was starting to worry that you were regretting letting me stick around."

He picked up his mug again. "Right now I'm definitely mourning the days pre-Charlotte because I feel like absolute shit right now. What the hell did we drink last night?"

I leaned over and looked into his mug. "Now that you're past the halfway point I can say *I told you so*." I sing-songed. "Why you didn't take my advice and drink the water and take the Advil is beyond me. And for the record I totally drank your ass under the table too."

He downed the rest of his coffee. "Yeah yeah. Since

you're feeling so amazing why don't you do me a favor and make me something that'll get rid of this hangover? Don't you have some magical potion you can make me?"

"You probably won't like the answer but in my experience the best cure is lots of water. I'll grab you a big glass and a banana that can help too."

He dropped his head back on the chair and groaned. "You might be the death of me after all. How did I let you talk me into this?"

"There was no convincing necessary. You were game because you thought you'd win. I saw your competitive side come out last night." I chucked as I went inside to make myself another cup of coffee and get his hangover help.

FOUR

WARD

AS USUAL *NRG NIGHT CLUB* was packed. This kind of place used to be my scene but not anymore. I wouldn't usually come anywhere like this but I knew Charlotte was looking forward to a night of drinking and dancing.

I held the door open for her and the speakers boomed from inside the club.

The last couple days had actually been enjoyable— well after the hangover went away. I stocked up on bananas after that since clearly I'd be drinking more with Charlotte than usual.

As much as the hangover sucked I had to admit it was worth it. While I had been to work some I'd been spending less time in the office and more time just having fun. It'd been a long time since I'd done that.

My hand automatically went to the small of her

back without thought as she walked past me and we made our way over to a high-top table that had a reserved sign on it.

I pulled out her stool and she eyed me suspiciously as I sat down beside her. "Did we just steal someone's table?"

"No." I chuckled. "I know DJ Hale personally." I nodded to my brother who was having a blast as usual. My parents nearly had a coronary when they found out that being a DJ was his goal in life but he's actually really good at it and he's booked non-stop.

She looked up at him as well but just smiled. I guess she really didn't remember my last name as she didn't seem to pick up on the connection. She also didn't seem to notice the resemblance between us which I found odd since my brother and I could be twins.

"You ready to get your drink on Ward?"

I leaned over to tell her that she was going down when I caught a glimpse of a familiar blond figure in the corner. I kept my gaze trained in that direction waiting for her to turn around.

Charlotte followed my line of sight. "Is that fucking Dylan?" Her mouth dropped open. "And Mindy?"

"Looks like it."

Dylan looked in our direction and his eyes narrowed on me.

"Looks like your little boyfriend is jealous." How does this guy cheat on her and then have the nerve to give a shit what she does? It always boggled my mind how selfish people could be.

Charlotte turned back around to face me. "I honestly couldn't give a fuck how he feels. We're here to have a good time."

"You're right." A flyer on the table cause my attention and got me thinking. "I have an idea." I picked it up and showed it to her.

She squinted. "Win a couples getaway?"

"Yeah. Let's enter the contest and make them even more jealous." I knew how Mindy was and this would definitely piss her off.

Her smile didn't reach her eyes but she nodded anyway. "Oh, if you think that will help you get Mindy back then I will help."

I stared at her for a moment trying to read her expression.

"How do we sign up?" She snatched the flyer out of my hand and read it. "Perfect. At the bar. I need a drink bad so I'll go sign us up."

I watched as she walked away. Sometimes she was such an odd woman.

I couldn't stop my eyes from darting off in Mindy's direction. She seemed to be having a great time with Dylan. *Maybe I'm better off without her.* That was something I'd contemplated more than a few times recently. I just couldn't shake the egotistical bull shit that she chose to be with other guys when we were together. I couldn't help but question why and that took me back to feelings that I wasn't good enough.

Charlotte set a beer bottle in front of me breaking me out of my inner turmoil.

"All signed up." She sipped at one of the two drinks she'd brought herself. "I'm not sure why you want to do this. We're going to lose." Her jaw was tense as she continued. "We don't know shit about each other."

She was right but I didn't care. We'd be front and center stage for all to see including Dylan and Mindy. If I was being honest I was hoping more for Dylan to be jealous. I wanted that asshole to see what he'd fucked up. Charlotte was awesome and I didn't understand why anyone would cheat on her.

"We'll wing it. When are we up?"

She lifted the card up with the number four on it. "There weren't many people signed up so we're number four of four. They should be starting any minute."

Charlotte was quiet after that. I tried to get her to interact but she seemed to be people watching and from what I could tell she didn't so much as glance in Dylan's direction. Maybe she really was over him.

We'd watched the couples up on stage and I felt like I was a little prepared by the time our number was called and we approached the stage.

"Up next we have Charlotte Miller and none other than my big brother Ward Hale everyone. Give them a round of applause."

Charlotte's eyes darted to mine when she heard that Dalton was my brother. I just nodded.

Dalton winked at her and I wanted to punch him in the throat. He had no idea who she was to me so he needed to back the hell off. His smirk told me he was messing with me but I didn't care.

"So just in case you guys weren't paying attention. The way it works is we pull cards from this bowl and you guys have to do what's on the card. After you guys are done the audience will vote with applause which couple did the best. Are you ready?" He looked to me first then Charlotte and we both nodded our understanding.

He pulled a card from the bowl. "Balloon course." He snickered like he did when we were kids. "I can't wait to see this. Can someone please video this? I need it for Christmas dinner conversation."

"Fucker." I muttered under my breath. "Let's do this."

Charlotte looked confused.

"I take it you've never seen this before sweet

cheeks?" Dalton came over put his arm around Charlotte. "Let me explain." He walked her over to the other side of the bar. "You'll need to pop a balloon at each station." He stood beside a mattress on the ground. "Here Ward will lay on his back and you'll have to lay on top of him to pop the balloon between your bodies." He moved to a chair and sat down. "Here you'll need to straddle his lap and again pop the balloon between you." He looked over at me. "Should we demonstrate?"

I shook my head as I glared at him.

"Can you guys see the smoke billowing from Ward's ears? It's quite easy to get him going." He walked over to an x marked on the ground. "Here you'll bend over and touch your toes while Ward plows into you from behind to break the balloon."

I walked over to them and wanted nothing more than to smack the smirk right off of him. I leaned over to whisper in Charlotte's ear. "Do you see why I like my brother-in-law better than him?

She giggled. "I think he's funny."

Of course she did. Everyone always thought he was. I clapped my hands together. "We got this."

We got ready in our positions.

Dalton started counting. "One. Two. Three. Go!"

Charlotte ran toward where I was laying on the mattress holding the balloon against her stomach. She belly flopped onto me and we popped the balloon on the first try.

I picked up a new balloon that was on the floor and we both ran to the chair where I positioned the balloon at my crotch. Charlotte jumped on top of me and straddled the balloon but it wouldn't pop. She bounced up and down as she gripped my shoulders. We were both laughing hysterically and finally got it after ten bounces.

She ran to the x and bent over.

"Give her Ward." My brother taunted.

I ran over to her, positioned the balloon against her ass and gripped her hips and then rammed into her popping it on the first try.

Charlotte got up and jumped into my arms. "We rock!"

My arms went around her waist and I spun her around.

"What's next?" I shouted to my brother excited for what we could do now. This was actually really fun.

He dipped his hand into the bowl and pulled out another card before he burst out laughing. "Can't wait to see this."

My stomach knotted wondering what it could be.

"This one is going to be ah-ma-zing folks. So we're going to play a portion of 6 songs that have popular dance moves. We will then play the song again while you *perform* said dance moves." He couldn't contain his laughter knowing I was never going to live this one down.

Charlotte leaned over. "I got this."

"Oh and you *both* have to get some right. It can't just be you Charlotte shaking that fine ass of hers." He dropped the card onto the table. "Let's move the mattress out of the way so you can get your *groove* on."

I felt like I was going to be sick. It's not that I didn't know *how* to dance but I hated dancing where anyone could see.

"Let's start off with a warmup. This one doesn't count though." He started playing *Stayin' Alive.*

I swallowed hard as Charlotte looked at me.

He turned the music off. "You ready guys?"

I nodded although I wasn't.

He started the song again and we both began dancing. It was simple enough so I got through it without hurling all over.

He went right into another song this time it was *Macarena.*

Charlotte hip checked me. "Ready?"

I nodded. He played it again and we both started to do the Macarena dance. Either the alcohol I'd consumed had started to kick in or I just didn't seem to care by then. The crowd was cheering and Charlotte had a huge smiled on her face.

The next couple songs were ones I had heard but didn't know they had a dance so Charlotte was on her own for *Single Ladies* and *Teach Me How to Dougie*. I watched mesmerized as Charlotte moved her hips to the music. She seemed to know every move.

When *Watch Me* came on everyone went crazy and did the dance with us. I was a little mortified I knew that one.

"Well shit. I wasn't expecting you to know *any* of those Ward. So I definitely applaud you." Dalton clapped and everyone joined in. He pulled out another card and this one I wasn't expecting at all. "Show us your most passionate kiss." My brother had no comment on this one as he watched us for a reaction. "

Charlotte turned to me with her shoulders squared. "We can do this. Just pretend I'm Mindy."

She looked up at me with a serious expression. I wasn't sure pretending would work and that was because in that moment I realized I *wanted* to kiss Charlotte not Mindy. My hand cupped her face as I slowly moved in.

Her eyes closed just before our lips touched and her breath hitched. The moment our mouths collided the room went silent and we were the only ones there. I threw everything I had into that kiss including feelings I hadn't even known existed.

She pulled back before I was ready. My eyes slowly

opened and found hers averting mine. I wanted to look into those green depths of hers but it didn't look like that would happen.

"Dayum…" Dalton broke me out of my thoughts. He was quickly becoming one of my least favorite people. "Did anyone else feel like they were intruding on a moment there?" He wiped his brow. "I have to admit that was hot bro."

I had to agree with him on that one but from the way Charlotte was ignoring me I wasn't sure she'd agree.

"All right now that we all need an ice-cold shower let's finish this off." He pulled the last card out of the bowl. "This one is easy enough. How did you two meet?"

I leaned in and whispered to Charlotte. "I got this."

She turned and looked up at me questioningly but I just smiled down at her.

I took the mic my brother held out. "I won't lie it was an unfortunate event that brought us together. Two people who we cared deeply for and trusted broke that trust in a way that no one should but I can't even be bothered to care anymore because it brought you into my life." I'd started off talking to the audience but had turned my attention to Charlotte. I took a deep breath and chose the corniest thing that came to mind. "So now I'm calling it a Christmas miracle."

Charlotte burst out laughing. The exact reaction I was hoping for.

"We haven't known each other long and I know we are on borrowed time but my life is better having known you no matter where we end up."

I leaned in and pressed my lips to hers for a moment before pulling back and speaking into the mic. "Now who needs a drink because I'm parched."

Dalton snatched the mic away. "Not so fast. Can I get all the couples up here please? It's time to vote."

We all lined up and the crowd voted by round of applause. When it came to our turn Charlotte took my hand squeezing it tight. The sound from the audience was deafening as they clapped, cheered and shouted for us.

"Looks like it's clear as day. Our best couple is Ward and Charlotte." He handed Charlotte an enveloped. "You've won an all-inclusive vacation to Mahona Island and you leave tomorrow." He kissed her cheek and a growl escaped my throat.

Charlotte turned to me with a huge smile on her face. "Holy shit we won." She jumped into my arms and wrapped her legs around my waist. "We really won."

For the first time since we started this contest I looked over at Mindy. I had forgotten she was even in the room. She was glaring at the two of us up here and the satisfaction I'd expected to feel wasn't there. I felt… indifferent.

"We didn't just win Char. We kicked ass."

She pulled back and cocked a brow. "Did you just call me Char?"

"Yeah I guess I did. Is that a problem?"

She smiled. "Nope not at all."

I kept one hand around her waist and raised the other in the air. "Shots on me."

The whole club erupted and the bartenders immediately got to work on making the shots.

"I'm actually really excited to get away. I know I'm on vacation but I feel like I need this. I think it'll be good for both of us." Charlotte kissed my cheek and hopped down. "I also think I want one of those shots and then we dance." She poked me in the middle of my chest. "And that includes you. Now that I know you can shake that ass of yours there's no excuses."

I shook my head but she wasn't paying any attention to me as she was already headed in the direction of the bar pulling me behind her. She didn't seriously think we were taking this trip did she? I couldn't leave the resort for a whole weekend. And what's this shit about dancing? I better take a few of those shots myself if I was going to do any more dancing.

FIVE

CHARLOTTE

WARD ROLLED his eyes as he looked over my shoulder. "Don't you have some songs to play or something?"

Laughter rang from behind me and a large hand landed on my shoulder.

"Ah big brother. Always so happy to see me."

Ward's eyes flicked down to his hand on my shoulder. "I'd be a lot happier if you'd get your hand off my girl."

It was my turn to laugh. "Your girl huh?"

His eyes went wide but he recovered quickly. "You know what I mean."

"Not really. I'm pretty sure we're trying to make some bimbo jealous tonight so she will take your ass back." I'd had quite a few drinks and was feeling pretty brazen so I turned to Dalton. "I think my job of making her jealous is done for the night. Do you want to dance with me?"

I saw Ward's jaw clenched out of the corner of my eye and Dalton smiled. "I'd love nothing more but Ward's right I have to get back to work but I'll take a raincheck on that one." He kissed my cheek and turned to walk away but stopped to look back at me. "If that was all for show then you two are in the wrong industry. You should be actors for sure because the way you two look at each other is like nothing I've ever seen." With that he sauntered off without looking back.

I picked up a shot off the table and took it back. It went down smooth and my body turned warm. I slammed the shot glass back down on the table.

Ward was watching me with a slight scowl on his face.

"Why are you such a stick in the mud?" I heard my words slur slightly but I didn't care. I really wanted to know what was up his ass.

I stepped forward and I looked up at him before running my hand down his cheek. "You know you're a great actor."

He shook his head.

"No really. You almost had *me* believing you up on stage. You were—" I leaned in closer to him. "—*very* realistic." I pointed in the direction of Dalton. "Even your own brother was convinced."

He stared at me for a long moment before his lips turned up into a beautiful smile. "I think you're a little drunk."

He was right but that was beside the point because I wasn't drunk on stage. That kiss felt real like really real. For an instant I'd let myself get caught up in the moment but ultimately nothing mattered because I was going back to New York and he would be here.

I let out a huge breath and decided I'd just have fun tonight. I reached out and took his hand. "Let's dance." Although he resisted it was for show because I was easily able to pull him into the crowd. We found an open spot and began to move. The music was somewhere between slow and fast making for some awkward movements. After a minute Ward wrapped his arm around my waist and pulled me flush against him. At first my body went rigid but I quickly loosened up and started to move to the music with him. I wasn't sure why he didn't like dancing because he was damn good at it. By the way he moved his body I would bet he was damn good in the—I stopped my thoughts before they went there. *No way Char. Don't even think about it.* I mean sure we could have amazing drunken sex but then tomorrow when it was uncomfortable I would have to live with him until I went home. So that was a big fat no.

The music shifted to a much slower pace and I

looked up to find a smirk on Dalton's face. *Bastard.* He winked and went back to looking at the screen in front of him. The song sounded familiar but I couldn't quite put my finger on it with the mixing he was doing but when the words to *Can't Fight This Feeling* started playing I burst out laughing.

Ward pulled back but kept his arms around me. "What?"

I placed my hand to my ear. "Can't you hear the words. Your brothers got quite the sense of humor with this song."

Ward paused for a moment to listen and then grinned. "Yeah he's *hilarious.*" He pulled me back in and started to move to the rhythm.

I let the words wash over me. REO Speedwagon was always one of my favorites. When the song ended I opened my eyes to find Mindy and Dylan walking out the door.

I hadn't even realized they were still here I was so wrapped up in my own world. "Looks like your plan may have worked." I nodded to the door.

Ward followed my gaze but quickly looked back at me. "Yeah I guess so. Drink?"

"Please." I followed behind him back to our table where we spent the rest of the night drinking and dancing and having a great time. When we got home

Ward actually followed my advice to stave off the hangover. Guess he learned that lesson quickly.

When the morning came I wasn't feeling one hundred percent but based on the amount of alcohol I consumed that didn't surprise me. I made my way downstairs to grab something to eat and order some coffee but Ward was one step ahead of me. He must have heard me coming because he handed me a mug that was filled with coffee just the way I like it. "Good morning."

I eyed him suspiciously. "You seem like you're feeling pretty good this morning."

"I didn't drink too much last night and I did your little routine before bed so I'm feeling great." He looked me over. "Not feeling so hot?"

"Not really but I'm super excited about seeing this other island." I grabbed a banana and sat down. "What time do we leave? I haven't even looked at the information your brother gave me."

Ward sat down across from me. "About that. I can't go."

He wasn't serious? "Why not? It's a vacation away. Name one good reason you can't go."

"I have work. I can't just leave the resort for an entire weekend during season." He took a sip of his coffee and sat back in his chair.

I leaned forward and gave him my best stink eye.

"Oh we're going. Don't think I didn't notice your last name matches that of the resort."

His brow rose.

"Yeah I'm not stupid. You aren't *just* the manager. So tell me again why you *can't* go away for two freaking nights. Plus you said yourself you've never been there so maybe you can get some ideas from their resort for yours." I crossed my arms and dared him to try and bull shit me.

"Fair enough. *Technically* I can go but I don't like to be too far in case shit hits the fan. It also looks like we've got a storm coming in."

I peeked out the windows and it did look a little dreary but nothing crazy. "Perfect. So it's settled."

He sighed but didn't respond. I spied the envelope on the console table by the door and went and snatched it up before sitting back down. I browsed through everything. "Looks like we have to be at the airport in four hours. Even if it's raining we can still relax and just hang out. Right?"

He looked at me but stayed silent.

"Come on Ward please!" I whined. "I have nine more days here and I want to make the most of it. We will be back Christmas eve so you won't miss any festivities. Please!" I gave him the cutest puppy dog eyes I could muster.

He got up and put his mug in the sink. "You're a

pain in my ass you know that?" He headed toward the stairs without another word.

"Where are you going?"

He paused mid-step. "Some of us aren't on vacation—

"Yet." I interrupted.

He rolled his eyes and shook his head. "—anyways. I have things to take care of. I can't just up and leave without letting people know and putting some things in place."

I squealed and ran over to hug him. "Thank you."

He hugged me back. "Yeah yeah. Pack light. It's only two nights."

I ran past him up to the room to pack. I couldn't wait.

———

THE PLANE TOUCHED down at the Mahona Island Airport in less than an hour and we stepped out onto the tarmac to the same clear skies without a cloud in sight. There was a car waiting to take us to the resort. I felt like a princess, there was even champagne in the backseat.

I took a sip of the glass that Ward handed me. "This is exactly what I was born to do."

"What's that? Get wasted in the back of limousines?"

I back handed him in the stomach. "No. A life full of luxuries."

"Really? I never pegged you for a girl who wants to be wined and dined."

I eyed him over my glass. "I'm not sure if I should be offended by that comment or not."

"Definitely not. It was meant as a compliment. You don't seem to be high maintenance like the majority of the women I come across. It's refreshing actually." He set the bottle in its holder.

He was right about that I was far from high maintenance. "You're right. I don't *need* these things all the time but every once and a while it would be nice to be treated like a princess." I shrugged.

It didn't take long to arrive at the Resort. The entrance was nice but didn't have that wow factor Hale Court Inn had. We approached the check in desk where we were greeted by a young woman who didn't even bother to look up at us until she heard Ward's deep voice. That got her attention and she then couldn't seem to look away.

When she found out we were the winners she called someone who came out immediately. George introduced himself and explained he was to be our personal support for the weekend there and to reach out any time we needed anything. He took us to our room which was on the fifth floor of a walk up. My legs were burning by the time we reached the door. Our bags had already been placed inside and George left us to explore the room and enjoy the wonderful spread of goodies they'd provided.

I flopped back onto the bed and sprawled out. "My legs feel like I just walked a mile."

"Do you really never work out? Your body says otherwise." He wasn't looking at me when he said those words and for that I was grateful because he would've seen me turn beet red.

I really didn't work out. "I *have* worked out but I don't. I can't seem to do it. I know one day it'll catch up to me but for now I'm enjoying life without strenuous activities that I don't enjoy."

I hopped off the bed and walked out onto the balcony. The view was stunning but it wasn't the same being this high up. In the city the best view is from a skyscraper but when you have nothing obstructing your view I like to be as close to the beach as possible.

Ward stepped up beside me. "So far I don't see any ideas I would take back to the inn."

"I have to agree with you there. I'm far from impressed but that food looks amazing but that may be because it's way passed lunch time and I haven't eaten anything but a banana today."

Ward shook his head. "I told you to eat before we left for the airport."

I sat down on the sofa and started picking at the fruit and sweets that were laid out for us as I looked around the room. It honestly looked like every other hotel I'd stayed in before.

"Notice anything that's missing?" he asked as he sat down beside me.

I looked around again. "No."

He popped a grape in his mouth. "There's only one bed."

I peered over at it and shrugged. "I mean we did win a *couples* weekend away. Did you expect them to give us two beds?"

"No I guess not. I'll take the couch though."

I eyed the couch which was more like a love seat. "Ward you cannot sleep on this."

"Sure I can." He laid across my lap with his legs hanging clear off the end.

My body shook with laughter at his ridiculousness. "Yeah that looks really comfortable. Hey how about we both sleep on the sofa together since it's so restful?"

"Don't be ridiculous. You're much too short for this."

I rolled my eyes. "We're both adults. I don't think anyone needs to sleep on the couch. We can share the bed. What's the issue?"

He sat up abruptly and looked between me and the bed a few times.

"You look like a deer caught in headlights. I don't bite I promise." I wasn't sure why this was such a big deal. "Have you never slept with a woman that you aren't actually *sleeping* with?"

He shook his head. "Nope. I can honestly say I haven't."

"Well there's a first time for everything. Now stop being a pussy." I slapped his leg and shoved the rest of my brownie into my mouth. "Now that's something you should be offering at your resort because those are *amazing*."

He took a bite of one and I watched as his eyes closed slowly and he purred. "Okay I'll admit it. Those are really good."

I grabbed another. "I should just move to the island and you could hire me to help you with these very important decisions."

SIX

WARD

FOR A MOMENT I allowed myself to visualize Charlotte in my life permanently. "Do you ever think about leaving New York?"

"I always pictured myself there but I think that's only because it's all I've ever known. I'd never traveled further than a few hours from home until this vacation. Since coming here all I've thought about is living somewhere else. Being on the beach and in the sun feels more like home than I've ever felt. It truly isn't realistic for me to up and move to a completely different country so my thoughts have been on Florida maybe. Anywhere that I don't have the winter." As she spoke she got a faraway look in her eyes and a huge smile on her face.

The thought of moving away from home gave me

anxiety. "I can't ever imagine leaving. Won't you miss your family and friends?"

"That's because you literally live in paradise. I'll miss my family and a few friends and honestly it's a lot to think about but I feel like it's time for a drastic change in my life." She shrugged. "Enough talk about my life outside of this vacation. It's a little depressing to think of going back to a gloomy winter in New York with no sunshine."

I frowned. "No sun?"

"Okay I might be exaggerating a little but our winters can get very grey and gloomy."

"That sounds miserable." I picked up a pamphlet off the table and browsed through it. "Let's go back to living in our bubble then." I turned the brochure around for her. "How does a dinner show sound?"

"That sounds great to me. When does it start?" She learned in and read it over. "Oh my God a trapeze artist?" She snatched the paper out of my hand. "We need to get a good seat so let's get ready now. It starts in two hours. "She hopped off of the couch and pulled me up with her.

"Yes ma'am."

I let her use the bathroom first and then I took my turn. When I walked back out to the living area I stopped short the moment I saw Charlotte's reflection in the mirror. She looked stunning. Her long brown hair was down and swept to the side and the little white dress she was wearing clung to her body like a second skin.

"Do I look okay?" She looked completely unsure of herself and I wasn't certain how that was possible.

I looked her up and down. "You look…perfect." My voice lowered to a whisper and I cleared my throat to try and cover it up.

Her cheeks pinked as she walked over to me. She reached up and smoothed out the collar of my polo shirt. "You look pretty good yourself their Ward."

The urge to lean down and kiss her seemed to be a constant since my lips had touched hers last night. My eyes flicked down and then back up.

"We should get going." She didn't make a move though.

I smiled thinking maybe her thoughts were in line with mine. "We have time."

"Yeah." Her voice was breathy. I loved that I was having the same effect on her as she had on me.

I cleared my throat again. "But you're right. We should probably go so we can get a good seat." As much as I wanted to walk us backward until we both fell to the mattress I knew that was a bad idea. If she lived here I wouldn't give it a second thought but there was something about her that told me I couldn't have her just once and I didn't think it was fair to cross that line knowing there was nothing on the other side for us.

She backed away and picked up her shoes before slipping them on and tying the straps up her legs. "I'm really excited. I've always wanted to go see *Cirque du Soleil* and this seems like it's the closest I'm going to get to it because the tickets for that show are way out of my budget."

"Well let's get going then." I followed behind her as we headed to the show. We were one of the first few to arrive. We asked the host where the best seat was. I slipped him a fifty-dollar bill and he seated us in a roped off section of the theatre.

Her jaw fell open when she saw where we were being seated. "Oh my God Ward. This is amazing." She threw her arms around me. "Thank you."

We sat in our seats and she looked around in awe. "This place is huge." She leaned in. "But I prefer the inn. The intimacy of your place is what appealed to me. It's luxurious in all the right ways but relaxed and quaint as well. From the moment I saw it in the magazine I just *had* to come visit."

I nodded. "Thank you. I've worked hard to bring that balance to our resort. This place may lack in accommodations but it has some crazy amenities."

"Very true. I think the weekend will be great

though and since the room is meant for sleeping..." her cheeks flushed and she looked down for a second. "... well for us at least it doesn't matter that it feels like a bland hotel room. I don't think we'll be spending much time up there otherwise."

I needed to think of anything other than being in bed with her. Maybe getting plastered tonight was the best idea. I could stumble back to our room and pass out instead of lying there beside her thinking of all the naughty things I want to do to her.

A waiter approached and handed each of us a menu. "How about a pre-dinner drink?"

"Please." I ordered two for myself and Charlotte eyed me skeptically. I just shrugged. It's not like I could admit my inner thoughts to her.

She ordered her drink and once the server had left she leaned over placing her hand on my thigh to hold herself up. "Are you okay? You seem a little...tense."

My body was certainly tense right now. The simple touch of her hand on my thigh had me on full alert. I let out a huge breath and reached over to put my arm on the back of her chair feigning nonchalance. "I'm great." I picked up the dinner menu trying to distract myself. "This all sounds delicious."

She stared at me for a moment before picking up her own menu. "Oh wow it does. I'm sorry I made you come out so early I really just wanted the best seats."

I looked around us and noticed quite a few people were piling in. "I think you had the right idea I'm sure it'll get packed in here plus we can have some drinks and talk before the show starts."

"True." She smiled at someone behind me. "Speaking of drinks."

Just in time.

We talked about work and life in general but kept things late. Her life back in the U.S. sounded fun and carefree and the more I thought about my life before Charlotte it was...bland. It basically consisted of work and home.

"How old were you when you started to work at the inn?"

I considered her question for a moment and realized it'd been longer than I thought. "We all worked there growing up but I was the only one who stayed. My brother told my parents early on that he wanted to be a DJ. They both laughed at his career choice but he was determined to make a name for himself. My sister only ever wanted to be a mom. She's been with her husband since they were in high school and she has no desire to work outside the home. So after high school I went to college part time and took business and hospitality courses. I started working there full time 10 years ago and my parents officially retired two years ago and handed me the reins on my thirtieth birthday."

Her eyes went wide. "Oh wow. That seems like a lot of responsibility at such a young age. So you literally run the place?"

I chuckled. "I couldn't say that. We staff over 50 people and I have an amazing management team that I depend on. Especially when I have crazy New York women coming to stay with me and forcing me to spend days on end away from the office."

"Oh does that happen often?" She deadpanned.

I shrugged. "No more than once or twice a year."

"In all seriousness I hadn't thought about it much but I assumed you worked for your family's business so you could fuck off for a weekend. I didn't realize the responsibility of the entire resort was on your shoulders. I apologize for pulling you away so much." She looked down at her napkin and started to fiddle with it.

I reached over and lifted her chin to look up at me. "Don't apologize. I've had such a great time with you and you forced me to see that I don't have to be a workaholic. So I actually should be thanking you." It was true. I barely thought about work when I was with her. We truly were in our own little bubble. I wasn't looking forward to when it finally bursts.

She squared her shoulders. "You're welcome." Her

smile was wide as she looked at me. "I've had a lot of fun with you too."

Our conversation made the time fly by and before we knew it they were bringing out the first course. The music and lights kicked in almost immediately and I watched Charlotte's face become animated. I imagine that was what a child looked like the first time they walked into Disney World.

I tried to watch the show but I couldn't keep my eyes off of her.

When the third course came I hadn't touched any of my food. She looked over at the three plates in front of me. "Are you not hungry?"

"Not really." I lied and my stomach growled but thankfully the music drowned it out.

She set her fork down. "Are you enjoying the show?"

"It's amazing." I honestly hadn't seen a quarter of it so all I could do was hope she didn't ask me anything specific.

She smiled. "Isn't it? I've never seen anything like it." She pointed to her steak. "You need to try this." She moaned around a mouthful.

I knew if I didn't eat now I was going to regret it later. So I took my first bite and it really was great. I ate quickly and even downed the first two courses.

"Not hungry huh?" She laughed.

Before I could respond the lights changed and the music grew darker and Charlotte became entranced again. I went back to watching her instead of the show and didn't stop until dessert was placed in front of me.

"Oh my God. Coconut is my favorite." She popped one of the coconut ice cream balls in her mouth and her eyes closed in what could only be described as ecstasy. "I've literally died and gone to heaven Ward."

I picked one up and ate it. "Wow that is really good. Maybe we need to step up our desert game when I get back."

"Can you do that immediately so I can help with the taste testing?"

I chuckled. "I'll see what I can do but I can't make any promises."

They announced the finale and this time I watched the show. It certainly was a hypnotic performance once I started to watch.

After the final notes were played and the house lights came back up we took our drinks to go and decided to walk the beach.

"Thank you so much for taking me tonight. It was truly a night I'll never forget."

I looked over at her the moonlight illuminating our way. "I wouldn't have missed it for anything." I would cherish tonight as well although for reasons far different than Charlotte.

She looped her arm with mine. "So what's on the agenda for tomorrow?"

"Tomorrow they have us going horseback riding in the afternoon and then dinner on the beach."

She hummed and rested her head on my shoulder. "That sounds nice."

We walked along the shore in a comfortable silence for a while.

"You know what we should do tomorrow? We should watch the sunrise on the beach. I've never seen the sun rise before and I bet it's super pretty here."

I stopped short. "How have you *never* seen a sunrise?"

She shrugged. "I don't know. I guess because I was always sleeping."

I bumped her shoulder with mine. "Smartass. Well we should probably get to sleep if you want to wake up at six."

"Good call."

We headed back to the room and the moment we opened the door it hit me again that we only had one bed. I didn't say anything as I took off for the bathroom. I took my time washing my face and brushing my teeth. When I couldn't hold off anymore I stepped through the door to find Charlotte in a tiny tank and panties.

She stood there looking sheepish. "I didn't bring anything to sleep in."

I swallowed hard. "I didn't either. I can honestly sleep on the sofa. It's really not a big deal."

"Don't be ridiculous. I was just explaining myself." She smirked. "I didn't want you to think I was trying to seduce you in my *sexy* outfit." She laughed.

I looked her up and down slowly. There would be zero seduction required. It was already taking everything in me not to take full advantage of her as it was and a man can only take so much.

I cleared my throat a few times. "It's your call but I only have boxers to wear."

"I think I can survive." She walked passed me and closed the bathroom door behind her.

I stripped out of my clothes and laid them on the back of a chair before grabbing my phone to set the alarm. As I was heading back to bed Charlotte walked out of the bathroom and slammed right into my chest. I gripped her hips to steady her and her hands landed on my shoulders.

"Crap. I'm sorry I wasn't paying attention." She looked up at me and her eyes flicked to my lips.

I snapped out of it and stepped back. "It's fine." I forced a smile. "Ready for bed?"

She looked toward the bed and then back at me. She seemed to be just as unsure as I was. "Yep." She faked a yawn and stretched her arms up high causing her barely there tank top to ride up exposing the bottoms of her breasts.

Lord help me get through this night.

She hopped into bed and I shut off the lights before carefully climbing under the covers. My body was as close to the edge as possible and I was as stiff as a board. I was going to wake up feeling like I'd slept on that sofa.

I could hear Charlotte tossing and turning and all it did was amplify my feeling of restlessness. I thought to myself that if she'd just fall asleep it would be quiet and I could pretend she wasn't there. Then maybe I could fall asleep as well.

I laid there for what felt like hours without moving. I evened out my breathing as well as counted sheep.

She let out a loud sigh. "Are you awake?"

I debated on staying quiet but decided against it. "Yes."

"I can't sleep." She turned and although I could barely make out her silhouette in the dark I could tell she was facing me.

I rolled over to face her as well. "Should I sing you a lullaby?"

"I know you can't see me but I'm rolling my eyes at you right now."

I did the same but didn't tell her.

"Could we play a game?"

Girls were so weird. "What kind of game can we play in bed in the dark?"

She giggled. "Well…" She paused for a moment. "Just kidding. Umm…maybe just talk then?"

Talking I could do as long as she stayed on her side of the bed and the conversation steered away from anything of a sexual nature then I was safe. "Sure. Maybe you can bore me to sleep."

She slapped my arm. "Hey! I'm not boring."

"I was just kidding. Tell me where you see yourself in five years?"

She groaned and rolled onto her back. "Ugh! Well the answer days ago would've been married and probably having my first kid by then. But now I don't know. If I had to choose right this second I'd say that I would be living in Florida and happy. Possibly in a relationship but I'm perfectly content being single so maybe just a fuck buddy or two."

Or two? What the fuck? I kept my thoughts to myself. "Sounds like a good plan. Do you see yourself in the same profession?"

She hummed. "I think so yeah. Maybe a bar right on the beach though. Not a club. I see something super laid back. Yeah I like that. Sounds perfect. What about you? Where do you see yourself in five years?"

"I honestly haven't given much thought about the future but like you my world is a little different as of recently but if I had to say right now I would guess I'd be in the same boat as I am now. My life would revolve around work. I don't see marriage or kids in the future with how things have been going."

She sat up suddenly. "No!" He hand rested on my shoulder. "You can't go back to that. There has to be something more for you. Do you *want* to get married and have kids?"

"I do but let's be honest. When you leave I won't be living this carefree lifestyle I have been. It's different with you. I'm sure I'll go right back to my old ways."

It was upsetting to think about her leaving and my life going back to being a workaholic but I think that was my unfortunate reality.

"You need to find someone that makes you *want* to spend time away from the office. Clearly you don't take time off for yourself but you took pity on me and have been taking a ton of time out of your day for me. It's worth it for the right person. You just need to find her."

Yeah I needed to find someone like *her*. If she weren't from the US than maybe she'd be *the one*.

"Maybe you're right. Okay so I'll find the one and maybe we'll be married and on our way to kids too."

"Do I get to come to your wedding?"

I smirked and shook my head. "Sure."

"Yay! You'll have to pay because let's be honest I won't be able to ever afford to come back here again." She laid back down facing me.

We continued our talk about hypothetical futures and eventually we passed out.

SEVEN
WARD

WHEN THE ALARM woke me at six I had a small hand splayed across my chest and a leg up against mine. I opened my eyes but only moved to turn off the alarm. I didn't want to wake her just yet.

I laid there still and silent listening to Charlotte's breathing for a few minutes before I had to wake her.

"Char." I whispered and her eyes fluttered open slowly.

She turned to look at me and smiled. "Hey you."

"Morning."

She lifted up and rested her chin on my chest as she looked up at me. Her hair was a mess and her eyes were sleepy but she looked beautiful none the less. Well she always looked beautiful but there was something about how natural she looked right now. Her hair was messy but she didn't seem to care.

"You survived sleeping in the same bed as a woman I see. It wasn't that bad was it? How'd you sleep?"

Once I got tired it wasn't that bad it was before that that was tough. "I slept great after you finally stopped talking."

"Shut up. You talked way more than I did last night. You wouldn't shut up. I almost fell asleep a few times on you."

I flipped her over and hovered above her. "You're such a brat you know that?"

She didn't respond instead she just stared up at me. I looked down and realized the position I'd put us in. I was straddling her small frame wearing nothing but boxers and although it was dark I could see her nipples were hard through her barely there tank she was wearing.

"We should really get going." I climbed off the bed. "We only have about twenty minutes before the sun starts to rise."

She jumped up too and I watched as she slipped on a pair of jean shorts and a tee. I stepped into some shorts and a shirt and we headed downstairs. The coffee shop was open so we stopped in and grabbed one on the way.

We found a spot on the beach and sat down beside each other in the sand. When the sun started to peek up over the horizon I wanted to sit behind her and wrap my arms around her. The moment seemed to call for it but I refrained.

Her hand gripped my arm and she leaned into me. "It's beautiful." Her voice was nothing but a whisper as she watched the sunrise.

I looked over at her and smiled. "It sure is."

When the sun had fully risen she turned to me and wrapped her arms around my neck. "Thank you."

"You're welcome."

She kissed my cheek and pulled back. "You really have changed my life you know? This vacation went from the worst it could've been to something far better than I could've ever imagined and we barely know each other. You took me in when you didn't have to and I've experienced so much that I would've never otherwise. So I am forever grateful for you being so selfless."

"I'll admit that at first it was all in the name of the job. I never want a customer to leave unhappy but it's been amazing since the first day. You're going to make some guy really happy one day. I need to find myself a Charlotte that'll take me on adventures back on the island."

Her smile was sad and she said what I'd been thinking all along. Well sort of.

"Too bad we live so far apart. I'd probably maybe only a little bit consider dating you."

I picked up a little sand and threw it at her legs. "Take that back."

She jumped up and started to run but I knew I could run faster. I took off after her as her laughter boomed. I caught up to her with little effort and picked her up and threw her over my shoulder before running for the water. I got us to a few feet deep and threw her in the air. She screamed and then went under.

She broke out of the water and she looked around until she found me and then splashed water my way. "You suck. I was only half joking."

"Half joking? Wow thanks. Well I was just trying to make you feel better when I said I needed to find my own Charlotte on the island because that would be a nightmare."

Her mouth hung open in mock horror and her hand went to her hip. "Okay for real though you aren't *that* bad when you're having fun. I'd totally date you."

"Fine I'd totally date you too but I need *my* Charlotte to allow me to go to work at least a few hours a day because this whole not going to work at all thing doesn't run the resort."

She tsked me. "Oh please. We both know you aren't that important. You haven't gotten one emergency call since we've been here. They don't really need you there. That place runs like a well-oiled machine just fine without you."

"Sure I have competent staff because I hired and trained them but there are things that are piling up that no one else can do."

She smiled up at me. "Ah well you get to spend time with me so it's all worth it. When I leave you'll be so depressed and sad that you'll throw yourself into your work because life outside work won't ever be the same again."

I rolled my eyes. "Don't be so dramatic. You're going to be the one roaming the streets of New York lonely and cold and then you'll move to Florida to find the beach and sun but it won't be the same because it was me that you wanted all along."

She burst out laughing. "Dream on. I'm going to be living it up in Florida. You'll be begging to come visit."

"Yeah yeah." I really didn't want to think about how I was going to feel once she was gone. Maybe I just needed to take Mindy back and fall into my old life. I didn't really care about her but when we spent time together it was all right. I'd be settling for sure but at least I would have someone to come home to. Ugh that sounded pathetic even to me.

After our swim we got out and headed back to get out of our wet clothes and shower. I stood in the doorway of the bathroom and looked at her and deadpanned. "I can't allow you to join me in the shower. I know you want to date me and all but I cannot allow that to happen. I'm sorry."

She tried to whip me with her towel but I closed the door before she reached me. "You're an asshole Ward you know that?" She banged on the door. "Remember you said it first."

We both got ready before having a short nap—fully clothed.

Charlotte stretched and groaned. "I really needed that. Getting up at six am sucks donkey balls. I don't know how you do that every day."

"It was just habit. It seems you broke that on day one though. You ready for some food? I'm starving."

We hadn't eaten at all and we were due to go horseback riding this afternoon so we took off for the buffet to eat so we would have enough time to settle our stomachs before we started bouncing around on the trails.

Charlotte sat down across from me and set her plate down. "I haven't been on a horse in so long. When I was in middle school I wanted my own so bad of course my parents refused but they used to drive me every weekend to a farm over two hours away to ride. I loved it so much but my mom lost her job and we could no longer afford it so we had to stop."

I was a little nervous about riding but I wasn't

about to admit that to her. "I've never been on a horse."

"Never? Well you're going to love it. It's so much fun. I hope they let us canter on the beach. You feel like you're flying."

I took a bite of my food and my insides flipped. The thought of flying on a horse made me feel sick to my stomach. I put on a fake smile. "I can't wait."

We sat out by the pool and did a little people watching for an hour before we met the excursion guide at the front lobby. We took a van to an off-site farm where we were introduced to all sorts of animals including a monkey named Herbert. I snapped a few pictures of Charlotte with him on her shoulder and the two of us with him standing on both our heads.

When it finally came time to mount the horses I shoved the fear down. I put my left foot in the stirrup and pulled up before swinging my right leg over. The horse—whose name was Chestnut—started to move and I almost lost my balance but was able to recover quickly and sit down in the saddle.

Our guide took hold of the reigns and held us still. He explained where we were heading on the map and he got onto his own horse before leading the way. It took a little getting used to and I'm not going to lie it hurt my nuts just a little but I got the hang of the movements and used my legs like I was told which eased the pressure some.

We winded down trails and finally ended up on the beach. We started off slow but quickly picked up pace and before I knew it we were racing down the coastline. I focused on Charlotte who was laughing and having a great time which eased some of my worry.

I let go of the anxiety and decided to have fun. Don't get me wrong it was still scary as hell but it was exhilarating at the same time.

When we finished up the ride and got off the horses my heart still felt like it was pounding out of my chest.

"That was so much fun." She took a sip of her water and blew out a breath. "Did you like it?"

I plastered on a smile. "I'm not going to lie that was terrifying but it was sort of fun too . Not sure I will be doing it again anytime soon though."

She ran her hand down the horses neck. "You are such a baby. How can this beautiful creature be scary?"

"How about because this massive animal was catapulting me down the beach at 20 kilometers an hour and if I needed to stop I would have had to throw myself off because otherwise I had no clue what I was doing."

Charlotte burst out laughing.

I pushed her shoulder playfully. "I'm glad you find my near-death experience amusing."

She tried to catch her breath but it was no use. "It's not that. It's the thought of you throwing yourself off the horse to save yourself that has me dying with laughter." She could barely get the words out through her fit of giggles.

I rolled my eyes and thanked the guides before climbing into the back seat of the van. Charlotte was still laughing when she sat down beside me.

"You're actually a little shithead. Like my niece might be more mature than you are and she's a toddler. We also teach her to never laugh at other people's misfortunes." I couldn't hold in my own snort.

"You're so full of crap. Had it been your buddy saying that you would've laughed your ass off."

She was right but I'd never admit it.

———

AFTER DINNER on the beach we changed into our swimsuits to take advantage of the swim up bar and a little time unwinding in the water.

I laid my head back against the edge of the pool. "It's nice to be at another resort where no matter what happens I don't have to fix anyone else's problems. It's a very calming experience. And swimming at night while most people are at the clubs or in bed with their kids, that was a good call on your part."

"It's definitely lightyears away from screaming children and a packed pool full of loud people." She lifted her cup to mine. "Cheers to a relaxing trip—other than the horseback riding—and new friendships coming from a bad situation."

I rolled my eyes but still clinked my glass with hers. "You're never going to let me live that down are you?"

She shook her head. "Honestly it's funny but it's also endearing because a grown ass man was scared of a horse and you admitted that to me. It makes me feel good that you trusted me with that information."

I shrugged. "I mean who are you really going to tell?"

"Anyone that'll listen."

That didn't surprise me in the slightest.

We'd been drinking for a couple hours when the siren sounded alerting us that a storm was coming and we needed to exit the water. Our feet hadn't even left the pool by the time the first drop fell and then a torrential downpour started. We left our towels and ran for cover.

"Why did we just run? We were wet from the pool anyway."

She shrugged. "Natural instinct plus there could be lightning coming."

Just as she said that thunder cracked and she jumped. "Looks like it's a movie night.

A movie night in sounded like some more relax time and I was game for that.

We changed out of our bathing suits and into our so-called pajamas and grabbed a blanket to cover up with on the couch. I'd honestly never been happy for a hot girl to cover up until that very moment.

"I think maybe tonight you out drank me because I'm a little buzzed. You must be gaining in tolerance since we've started hanging out."

I shook my head. "That's because it seems to be your life's mission to try and turn me into an alcoholic before you leave."

She didn't respond instead just grabbed the remote from my hand and started scrolling. "Oh my God we have to watch."

I looked up at the screen and smiled. "I mean it is Christmas eve in less than a few hours so it's only right to watch *The Grinch* in my opinion."

She squealed and pressed play before curling up into my side. I stiffened at first completely unsure of what to do but then settled my hand on her hip. *It was just a movie between two friends* I told myself.

The Grinch was one of my favorite Christmas movies of all time so I was sucked in immediately.

Near the end Charlotte's breathing evened out and

she began snoring softly. I guess the drinks had caught up to her. I finished watching the movie and turned off the television.

Charlotte looked like she was sleeping so peacefully that I didn't want to wake her.

"Ward." Her voice was groggy and quiet. I didn't respond because I thought she was still sleeping. Her head turned so she was facing me but her eyes were still closed.

She reached up and placed her hand on my cheek. Her eyes fluttered open and she stared up at me. "You're perfect."

I chuckled at what I assumed to be drunken words. "You aren't so bad yourself."

"But look at you." Her hand caressed my face. "You're so handsome and fun to be around. Why can't you live in New York?" Her bottom lip stuck out as she pouted. "Life isn't fair."

I hadn't realized she was this drunk. Can someone get more drunk in their sleep?

"We could be so good together. Don't you think?" She sat up suddenly and leaned in close.

I smiled back at her. Although she was clearly out of her mind right now I had to agree with her. "Yeah I think we could be."

My hand reached out and touched her face. "You're pretty drunk aren't you?"

She didn't respond instead she leaned in and pressed her lips to mine but pulled back quickly.

"I'm sorry." She dropped her face into her hands and shook her head. "I'm such an idiot."

I put my arm around her and pulled her into my side. "You're not an idiot. Honestly I'd love to see where things would go with us but we live eight thousand kilometers away from each other and you're leaving in a week."

She peeked out from behind her splayed fingers. "I can stay. I don't need to go home." She giggled.

"I think you're really drunk and have no idea what you're talking about right now."

She stared into my eyes for a few seconds and then her hands grabbed my face and pulled me towards her. This time the kiss started off soft but quickly became frantic. She positioned herself to straddle my lap and instinctively my hands gripped her hips. She moaned into my mouth and my tongue found hers.

I knew I needed to stop this before it was too late but her taste was quickly becoming one of my favorite flavors and I wanted more. My hands slowly roamed her body and came up to cut her breasts. She ground down on my thickening cock and let out whimper.

Fuck. Reluctantly I pulled back. She looked at me for a moment and then she climbed off my lap and stood from the couch. She stared at me again and her mouth opened for a moment but she closed it before turning and heading to the bathroom.

The door closed and I dropped my head back to the sofa and let out a loud breath. "Fuck!" What the hell was I supposed to do? First of all she was drunk and second of all she was leaving. I already had feelings for this girl there was no way I could sleep with her and let her walk away but I owed her an explanation.

After a few minutes I listened for any sound coming from the bathroom. I couldn't hear a thing so I knocked lightly. "Charlotte?"

"I'll be out in a minute. Just go to bed."

Just go to bed? Like I was ever going to be able to sleep tonight. I climbed under the covers anyhow and turned out the light. Within seconds I heard the door open and felt Charlotte as she climbed in on the other side.

EIGHT

CHARLOTTE

I CURLED up under the covers and turned away from Ward. My stomach churned when I thought of how I'd basically attacked his mouth.

Oh my God.

I turned my face into the pillow. I wanted to scream. The words I'd said came flooding back and I now wanted to smother myself.

What was I thinking?

How was I supposed to face him in the morning? The only saving grace was that in my buzzed and sleepy haze he'd thought I was actually drunk.

"Char?" His deep voice broke through the silence in our room.

I faked a yawn. "Mmhmm?"

The sheets rustled as he moved on the other side of the bed. "Are you awake?"

Clearly he knew I hadn't fallen asleep that fast. Although he did think I was drunk. "Uh-huh." I didn't want to speak in fear of saying something stupid yet again.

"Can we talk for a sec?"

There really wasn't much to talk about but if we must I'd rather do it while faceless in the dark. "Talk about what?" I decided to play it down like nothing had happened.

"Char I'm sorry." I could hear the pity in his tone.

I rolled onto my back and looked at the ceiling. This was the last thing I wanted was for him to feel sorry for me. "Ward there's nothing to be sorry for. I had a little too much to drink and made a huge mistake. I honestly don't know what I was even thinking. You and me?" I let out a little chuckle. "Can you even imagine?"

He let out a loud breath. "Really Char? Come on."

"Can we just let it go and forget it ever happened? We can wake up tomorrow and go on like I never made such a stupid move."

He stayed silent for a moment and then huffed. "Goodnight." He sounded annoyed but I didn't want to further the conversation by asking what his problem was.

"Night." I rolled back onto my side and looked out the window at the moon. I felt like a weight has been lifted. I had no business kissing him anyways. He'd taken me in and gave me somewhere to stay when otherwise I would have been completely screwed and I still have another week before my flight home.

Speaking of home I'd be heading back to New York which was another reason why nothing could or would ever happen between the two of us.

Sleep finally took me after what felt like hours but I tossed and turned all night long.

When the morning sun broke I felt like I had just fallen asleep.

"Charlotte?" Ward's voice was quiet as he pressed lightly on my shoulder to wake me.

I stretched my arms above my head but kept my eyes shut. "It's way too early."

He chuckled. "It's almost noon and we have to be at the airport in less than two hours. I thought maybe we could get some brunch before we head out."

I was scared to open my eyes but he sounded normal. Maybe last night was all just a bad dream.

Slowly I opened one eye to peek up at him. He was standing over me in only a pair of boxers and his hair wet. He looked like sex on legs. I closed my eyes again to clear my head of all the inappropriate thoughts.

"Come on." He yanked off the covers and I look up to find his gaze locked on my body. His throat bobbed as he swallowed. There was definitely heat in his eyes but last night proved he didn't want me regardless. I mean if a guy turns you down when there's no chance of a commitment clearly he isn't into you . No man turns down a fling, right?

I rolled out of bed and headed straight for the shower in hopes of getting my thoughts in order before breakfast. I could only hope that after last night he'd go back to being a workaholic and I'd have a quiet week in paradise alone before going home and putting this whole vacation behind me.

I'd forgotten to bring my clothes into the bathroom with me so I strutted out in my barely there towel to pick up some comfy clothes. I chose a pair of leggings and a fitted tank and grabbed my hoodie for the plane ride as it had been cold on the first flight.

I felt his eyes on me with every move I made and I couldn't shake the dreadful feeling that everything had changed.

Breakfast felt like business as usual. He seemed to be making an effort to keep things light but the way he now looked at me was...different. I couldn't describe it and most of the time I couldn't read his expression.

When our plane touched down back on Malgaho Island and we walked out onto the tarmac I finally felt like I could breathe again. Although we'd talked the entire way I was feeling claustrophobic in my seat. On the car ride back to the resort I stared out the window most of the time.

Ward finally spoke. "What do you want to do today?"

"You probably have a lot of work to do in the office after being away for so long. I don't need a babysitter so you can do your thing."

His face scrunched up in confusion. "Okay…" He drew out the word. "It's Christmas Eve so I was thinking—"

"Oh God. I totally forgot it's Christmas Eve. You most likely have even more to do and family shit. Don't worry about me. I've got my island Christmas all planned out. So I'll be doing my own thing anyways." I had the fakest smile on my face even though all I wanted to do was cry. Being alone on Christmas wasn't really something I'd planned on doing but at least I'd have the beach.

He stared at me blankly. "Really?"

"Yes of course. You didn't honestly think I'd be moping around for the holidays did you?"

He shook his head. "Well no. I thought—"

"I can't wait. Just me, myself and I. It'll be so relaxing when most holidays are stressful and crazy. I'll be living the island life." I was so full of shit.

He chuckled just as we came to a stop at the front entrance of the inn.

His door flew open and there stood Mindy. "Baby where have you been?" Her voice grated on my nerves as she leaned into the car and wrapped her arms around Ward. Her eyes locked on mine and smirked donned her face. "I've been trying to call you."

He hadn't mentioned her calling and honestly I hadn't seen him with his phone at all the entire time we were away.

He stepped out of the car and I got out on my side.

"I've been busy. What do you need?" He sounded a slightly irritated but I couldn't be sure.

I watched as she ran her hand down his arm. "What time do we leave for your parents' house tomorrow for Christmas?"

"Tomorrow?"

She tsked as she reached up and touched his cheek. "Yes. We are heading there for breakfast. What time are we leaving?"

"Mindy. I—"

I took my bag from the bellhop. "I'll see you later Ward." I didn't want to sit around and wait for him to finish his conversation with her. This was what he'd been waiting for all along right? Her to come crawling back.

"Charlotte wait." Ward's voice boomed.

I lifted my hand in the air without turning to face him. "It's fine I have stuff to do." I could feel the tears starting to sting the back of my eyes and I didn't want either of them to see me cry.

I picked up my pace as I headed straight for Ward's place. When I walked in the door I felt like an intruder for the first time. The tears finally fell and I slowly crumpled to the floor. *What was wrong with me?* I knew what this was. I didn't even like Ward. He was a stuffy suit that was not even my type. Sure he was good looking but even if we lived on the same continent who wants another workaholic anyways? Not me.

I wiped my tears away. Everything with Dylan had finally caught up to me so I gave myself a minute to calm myself and stop the pity party before I went to gather my things.

I packed up everything except for a few essentials that I put in my tote and put on my bathing suit. I didn't have a clue what I was going to do. I didn't want to call my parents on Christmas eve and ruin their plans with my sob story so I needed to figure my shit out.

I walked into the lobby to find Ward still talking to Mindy. His back was to me and her arms were draped around his neck. Her eyes lit up as she saw me with my bag. She had won in her eyes. Not that there was any competition. He wanted Mindy and that was that. There was also the small issue of me not living here. I handed my suitcase to the concierge who said he would keep it there for me and handed me a claim ticket.

I took one last look at them before heading to the beach. Now that I was homeless again and basically stranded I needed to figure this all out.

I found a little spot that was hidden and isolated from the rest of the beach and laid down in the sun. I had no clue what I was going to do but I knew I needed to think things through.

While I'd been lying on the beach for a few hours now I still had no idea how I was getting back home. I'd called my parents but when I spoke with them I couldn't bring myself to burden them with my issues.

I picked up my things and went back to Ward's place to change hoping he was still with Mindy. I breathed a sigh of relief when I found the house empty. I figured I would change and get some dinner and maybe drink myself into a stupor at the bar. It wouldn't fix my problems but it would make me feel better.

I walked out the front door and smack dab into Ward's chest. "Shit. I'm sorry. I wasn't paying attention."

His brow furrowed. "Where have you been? I've been looking everywhere for you."

"I went to the beach to relax for a bit." I shrugged.

He stared at me for a moment. "I would've went with you. I didn't have your number or I would've called you."

I smiled up at him. "That's okay. I know you're busy." I went to step around him but he grabbed my arm.

"Are you okay? What's wrong?"

I shook my head. "I'm fine. I'm just heading out. I will see you later." I didn't wait for a response. I just turned and walked away.

I needed those drinks now more than ever. I settled in at the bar and ordered a shot of tequila and two rum and cokes. I downed the shot immediately and the burn felt good.

"Double fisting it tonight?" Dylan's voice startled me.

I turned to find him standing before me. He pointed to the seat beside me. "May I?" He looked like shit which made me feel a little better.

"I guess." I picked up my drink. "Not like this vacation could get any worse."

He sat down and ordered himself a drink while I browsed the menu.

"Listen." He sighed. "I'm sorry."

I chuckled and rolled my eyes. "Yeah I bet you are."

"I just. Honestly there's no explanation I can give you that will make what I did to you all right. I just need you to know that I do love you. I was just scared that things were moving too fast and I wasn't ready for it."

I turned to him and found nothing but sincerity in his eyes. "Look. I get it. I'm genuinely over it."

He cocked a brow.

"I mean I'm hurt don't get me wrong but I'm over *us*. Clearly it wasn't meant to be. I think I got stuck in the routine of us and let things ride but I was never really *in love* with you. It took you fucking someone else with zero remorse to show me that. So..." I lifted my glass. "...cheers to you fucking Mindy."

He lifted his glass. "You must've had a really bad day."

"Yeah well can't win them all. Can you?" I clinked my glass with his and a tear fell. "I think I needed this conversation. So thank you."

He nodded. "So you still staying with Mindy's boyfriend?"

"Nope. I think she's going to be moving back in so I've been wracking my brain to figure out how to get home. I'm definitely regretting the whole no credit card thing now."

He rested his hand on my shoulder. "Let me pay for your ticket. It's the least I could do. I'd offer for you to come back to our suite but I have a feeling that's the last thing you want."

I looked at his hand on my shoulder with distain and he removed it but I thought about his offer. "You know what? That's *is* the least you could do for me after what you did."

"I deserve that." He pulled out his phone and started scrolling through. "Looks like the next flight would leave in about eight hours." He looked up at me. "You sure this is what you want?"

I nodded. I needed to go home and get back to reality. "Please."

I heard my phone ding and I saw the notification was from the airline.

He pulled me in for a hug. "I really am sorry."

"I know." I hugged him back taking comfort in his arms for just a moment.

We had a few more drinks and I downed a burger before deciding to head to the airport six hours early. I stood in the lobby debating on whether to say goodbye to Ward or not but in the end I felt that I needed a clean break. I'd never see him again anyway so what was the point in an awkward goodbye after last night's debacle?

I asked the desk clerk for a piece of paper and pen as well as an envelope and decided a note would be good enough. It was late so I didn't think he would get it until the morning anyway. I'd asked her to put it on Ward's desk after I was done.

I'd arrived at the airport with hours to spare. The flight was going to be twelve hours with one stop over.

By the time I'd arrive home it would be around dinner time Christmas day so I would definitely have to Uber home. Home. The word brought tears to my eyes as I sat at the airport. I didn't have a home. I was going to have to explain all of this to my parents and I wasn't looking forward to it.

By the time they announced our flight was starting the board I'd just finished a book I'd bought in the gift shop.

My stomach dropped when I heard my section being called. I hadn't realized until that moment that I'd been hoping that Ward would show up to stop me from leaving. I shook my head to myself. I was such an idiot. At least my subconscious was nice enough to bury it deep down inside so I wasn't impatiently waiting for someone who would never come.

The flight wasn't quite booked so the seats beside me were empty. I was able to put my feet up and put in my headphones with some elevator music in hopes that sleep would take me under.

Unfortunately for me two hours passed and no such luck but thankfully I remembered that I had some Benadryl in my bag that would knock me out for a while for sure.

———

THE COLD AIR hit my face as I walked out of the airport and I instantly missed the sunshine and salt air.

My Uber pulled up and I threw my luggage in the backseat with me to save time and get out of the frigid air.

The driver took off toward Dylan's place and I stared out the window. The flurries began to fall and Christmas music started to play from the stereo.

The driver cleared his throat. "Do you have someone special waiting at home for you this Christmas evening?"

I shook my head. "Nope. It's just me." My eyes met his sad eyes in the review mirror.

"I'm sorry."

I shrugged. "It's all right." Although now that I was home I wasn't feeling the slightest bit okay about it. "On second thought." I pulled out my phone and changed the destination address in the Uber app.

His screen lit up and he smiled. "Where are we headed now?"

"My parent's place." I knew they wouldn't care that I was showing up unannounced and although I didn't want to burden them with my problems I knew they'd be there for me and support me regardless.

"I'm glad you won't be alone for the holidays miss."

I felt a lot better knowing I'd be with loved once as well even under these circumstances.

Thirty minutes later we were pulling up in front of their building. I thanked the driver and made sure to give him a large tip for the holidays.

With my luggage in tow I trudged through the snow and punched in the code to enter the building.

My heart raced on the elevator ride up and by the time I stood in front of their door my heart felt like it was hammering out of my chest.

While I had my own key I decided to knock instead and waited with bated breath for them to answer.

"Coming." I heard my mother sing-song from the other side of the door.

When she opened it I lifted my hands up and smiled awkwardly. "Surprise!?" It came out sounding more like a question than an explanation.

"Oh my. Charlotte. Come here." She pulled me into her arms and I burst into tears. She allowed me a moment before pulling back and holding me at arms-length. "What's wrong my dear?"

I shook my head as the tears continued to fall.

"Come in and we'll get you some tea." She put her arm around me. "Samuel come her and grab Charlotte's suitcase from the hallway."

My dad rounded the corner and his face fell when he saw me crying. "Charlotte?"

I shook my head and he came up and kissed my forehead. My dad didn't do well with tears so he went off to grab my luggage.

"Start the kettle too please honey." My mom shouted over her shoulder.

I hadn't realized how much I needed to get everything off my chest until I'd finally unloaded it all onto her. I didn't leave anything out including my horrifying moments of weakness with Ward.

She set her mug down and placed her hands on my shoulders. "We'll get you all sorted. Dylan was always an asshole."

"Mom!" I scolded

She just shrugged. "I'm sorry but he was. I would have never told you unless I felt it was necessary. You were always too good for him and not in the your my daughter kind of way."

She was right now that I could look back on it but I hadn't seen it before. He'd done a great job at making me feel like I was beneath him and I was lucky to have him.

"So I was hoping to be out of Dylan's place by the time he returns home." I cringed at asking anyone to help me over the holidays.

My dad walked in and took a seat in his Lazy Boy. "I'll get a couple guys together and we'll have you out in a jiffy. You can stay in the spare room as long as you need."

I decided now was a good time as ever to tell them my newfound dream of living at the beach. "While I was at Malgaho Island I realized that the sun and the beach made me extremely happy like nothing I've ever experienced. So...I think I want to move to a warmer climate." I prepared for the blow back.

My mom raised a brow. "Oh wow! Does this have anything to do with that Ward fellow?"

I chuckled. "No it doesn't."

"Well maybe—"

I put my hand up to stop her train of thought. "I was thinking more along the lines of Florida or the Carolinas not a whole other country."

"Oh that sounds nice. Honestly honey as long as you're happy we're happy."

I sighed and slumped back into the sofa. "Thanks mom and dad. I believe I have a good plan in place now even though just hours ago it felt like my world was had completely crashed and burned."

"I'm glad we could help sweetie. We're always here for you no matter what."

NINE

WARD

VISIONS OF CHARLOTTE in Dylan's arms haunted my thoughts all night long. I was sure that's where she was last night and it pissed me off more than it should have. I told myself it was because he cheated on her and that she deserved better but I knew deep down that it was for more selfish reasons than that.

I also knew I needed to get out of bed and head to my parents' house but I couldn't find the motivation to do it .

Last night I tossed and turned hoping I'd wake up to find Charlotte had crawled into bed with me but no such luck. I checked the other room numerous times as well but she hadn't come home.

I knew I'd messed up but I also didn't know how else I should have handled it. I knew if I slept with

Charlotte that it would be different and at the end of it all she'd be gone regardless so why make things harder than they needed to be?

My phone rang and I rolled over to see Mindy's face on the screen. I declined the call immediately. I wasn't sure what part she hadn't understood yesterday but I thought I'd made it abundantly clear that it was over. I'd finally come to the conclusion that I deserved better. I deserved someone that I wanted to spend time with outside of the bedroom and Mindy was *not* her.

My phone rang again but this time it was my sister.

"Yes?" I dragged out the word.

She huffed on the other end of the line. "You better get your ass over here. If your niece asks where her Unkie War is one more time I might actually scream."

A smile spread across my face thinking about how Ariella always said my name. "Okay I'll get up."

"Get up? You mean to tell me you're still in bed? Are you sick?" The motherly tone in her voice was amusing.

I rolled my eyes knowing she couldn't see me. "Bye Kenz." I hung up before she could keep going.

I was kind of grateful breakfast got changed to brunch because I wasn't feeling the Christmas vibes today. Although I usually loved this day I wasn't in the holiday spirits.

After getting ready I stopped by the office on my way out to make sure everything was in order.

Tammy handed me my mail and I wished her a merry Christmas as I walked into my office to sort through everything—I was procrastinating doing the whole family gig.

An envelope on Hale stationery caught my attention. I set the rest aside and opened the letter.

Hey Ward,

I'm sorry to leave like this but I felt that it was best to head back to reality and allow you to get back to yours. Thank you so much for taking me in when I needed it most. I will forever be grateful for that.

I've enjoyed this time more than you'll ever know.

I'm really happy for you that things worked out the way you wanted with Mindy. I'd like to think that I had something to do with that since my amazing dance skills won us that contest.

Anyway, take care. If you're ever in New York look me up.

Take care of yourself,

Char

The panic in me was overwhelming. "Tammy! When was this left?"

Tammy peeked her head into my office. "Umm." She looked up at the ceiling. "Yesterday."

"Did you see when she left?"

She nodded. "Right after she left that a taxi picked her up."

Fuck. "Thank you."

She smiled and left the room.

She was gone.

I woke my computer up and checked on Dylan's room. He hadn't checked out yet.

"Tammy did she have anyone else with her when she left?"

She appeared in my doorway again. "Nope. It was just her. Everything okay boss?"

I nodded. "Yeah. I'm just trying to figure a few things out."

My mind raced with thoughts of last night. I'd given her time to calm down and then went looking for her. When I'd found her at the bar with her arms wrapped around Dylan I'd thought the worst. I should've gone to her.

"Ugh!" I stupidly thought that she was going to come back to the house and we could enjoy the rest of her vacation. I truly couldn't believe she'd left without saying goodbye. That seemed so unlike her.

I pulled out my phone and realized yet again that I didn't have her number. I pulled up Dylan's reservation again to see if Charlotte was listed but she wasn't. There was no contact information and I wasn't about to reach out to Dylan. I knew for sure that douchebag wouldn't help me out and I knew I couldn't hold my tongue if I did call him.

"Why the hell didn't I get her number?" I raked my hand through my hair in frustration and let out a loud breath. I didn't have time to sit around and dwell on things but I would find a way to contact her. Even if it was just to say goodbye. I think I deserved that much.

I grabbed the bags full of gifts and I walked out to the lobby. "Have a great shift and enjoy your dinner tonight." I called over my shoulder as I walked out the front door.

Dean, my driver, was waiting outside and opened the door for me. My parents lived less than 20 minutes away so we pulled up to their drive in no time.

Ariella came barreling out of the house and jumped into my arms.

"Hey beautiful. Did Santa bring you lots of presents?"

She nodded. "Come see." She wiggled out of my arms and took my hand pulling me toward the house. She didn't give me a moment to stop and say hi to anyone as we passed them in the foyer. I waved and said my hellos and barely kiss my mom on the cheek as I passed her.

We came to a stop in front of the Christmas tree and she tugged on my arm to pull me down to her level.

"Wook at da pwesents Unkie War." She walked around and pointed at all of them.

I chuckled. She never seemed to stop. Always go, go, go. "I see. He brought you lots of presents this year. You must have been an extra good girl."

Dean came in with my bags of gifts.

"More pwesents?" She placed both her hands on her cheeks as her mouth hung out in surprise.

I took the bags from him and tipped him before giving him the night off.

Ariella helped by putting all the gifts under the tree sporadically giving me time to greet my family.

I made my rounds and greeted everyone as usual. My mom was last but she gave the biggest hugs for such a small woman. She pulled back with a sad smile on her face. "You came alone?" Her voice was soft so that only we could here.

"Yeah Charlotte went home to spend the Holidays with her family." I smiled and kissed her cheek.

My brother slapped me on the back. "You must have scared her away somehow because you two had something special if you ask me."

Apparently, we weren't quiet enough. "I didn't ask you." I said through gritted teeth. I tried to calm myself knowing his words were meant as a joke but they stung. "Yeah we had a lot of fun but she lives thousands of kilometers away so it doesn't really matter does it?"

"If you ask me it sounds like it does matter."

I glared at him. "Again, I didn't ask you."

I was hoping my family wouldn't remember that I had asked about bringing Charlotte along for Christmas but no such luck. Good thing I had my niece to keep me occupied.

I scooped her up into my arms. She started talking a million kilometers a minute and I couldn't understand a word she was saying.

"Can we eat now that wards here? I'm starving." Dalton was practically whining. I was only 20 minutes late. I gave him the stink eye but he just laughed. He stopped on his way to the dining room and raised his hands in the air. "I have some post brunch entertainment for everyone at Ward's expense."

I rolled my eyes and shook my head. I had the longest fuse on any given day but today he was about to make me explode and it had only been a few minutes. If Charlotte were here with me I'd be laughing right along with him about the videos of the couples contest but I didn't want to see them. Not yet at least.

My mother headed straight for the kitchen and I followed behind to help. She always went all out. We had a buffet of every brunch food you could think of and then some. I helped her get everything into the middle of the table before we said grace and began to eat.

My sister was smiling at me like a loon. "We are going to do stockings and gifts after brunch instead of dinner. Jason has to work in the morning so we're going to head home after tonight. I hope that's okay with you."

I smiled. "Sure." I lied. I wasn't sure why but it bothered me more than it should. We didn't do breakfast today because of their schedule and now a difference in order of how we open gifts? In my thirty-two years we'd always opened stockings after breakfast and presents after dinner. Not once had it been different—until today.

My world felt like it was off kilter today and I thought being here and participating in the usual traditions would help but it's making things worse.

I looked up to find McKenzie still grinning at me.

"Why are you looking at me like that?" I wasn't sure why but it made me feel uncomfortable.

She looked at her husband and he nodded.

"I'm pregnant." She squealed.

My mom jumped up and practically ran around the table to hug her. Everyone congratulated them including myself. I should've felt joy for them but I couldn't help however feeling a pang of jealousy which shocked the hell out of me. The conversation shifted to all things baby for the remainder of our meal.

Ariella started getting restless as we finished up eating so we ate quickly so that she could start opening gifts.

I went through the motions with everyone smiling and laughing at the appropriate times but I felt like an outsider looking in on my own family.

My dad placed his hand on my back. "How's the Inn coming along?"

This was his way of asking me how I was doing personally without bringing up feelings because he wasn't *that* guy.

We talked for a good bit but it all seemed surface level.

"Who's Charlotte?" My sister asked as she held up a small gift. She must not have heard our exchange about her earlier.

I held my hand out. "Oh I forgot that was in there." I had bought Charlotte a small gift when I thought she'd be joining us today.

She handed me the box. "Is she someone special in your life?"

I knew she wasn't trying to pry and usually I'd be extremely forthcoming with McKenzie but the truth was I didn't know what to say. So I lied. "Nah, we're just friends. I'll Mail it to her when I get back."

"Mail it? Where does she live?" She seemed genuinely curious.

I sighed. "She lives in the US. She was staying at the Inn but she's gone now. She was supposed to be here today but she left to be with her family for Christmas. Nothing more to it."

"Keep telling yourself that brother." Dalton's voice continued to grate on my nerves.

I turned to find him grinning. "Can you not?"

He held up his hands in surrender knowing he'd pushed a little too hard.

We all sat there in silence. Everyone watched me as I watched Ariella continue to open her pile of presents.

My mom came up and patted my shoulder with a sad smile. I didn't want anyone's pity I could have a pity party for one when I got back home tonight.

But honestly I didn't know why I would need to. Yes she'd left but that was nothing new. She was always leaving. What was the big deal?

Who was I kidding? As much as I lied to myself she was more and although I always knew she was leaving deep down I had hoped that she wouldn't.

Wow! I was a complete moron.

I shook off the dread and vowed to enjoy the rest of the day with my family. It was Christmas after all and no one should be down on Christmas. I would figure everything out later.

————

MY PARENTS' house turned out to be a wonderful distraction after all. No further mention of Charlotte and although things turned out to be not as we usually did them it was a great day.

I opened my front door with a smile on my face but the moment I walked through it reality set in.

She wasn't here.

She wasn't coming back.

I needed to let her go.

Her gift burned a hole in my jacket pocket reminding me that I had no idea where she was right now and that I couldn't even mail it to her if I wanted.

I laid down on the couch and let my mind race with every scenario possible. Unfortunately no matter how things played out it didn't work.

Long distance wouldn't work. They rarely worked when the relationship had a great foundation and years under their belts. We didn't live hours away from each other we lived half a day's flight away from each other.

Moving here wasn't an option. I couldn't ask someone who I'd just met to move their life to another country thousands of kilometers away from her family.

My life was here with the family business and I

couldn't move no matter how much I wanted to go after her.

I felt like such a loser as I sat on my sofa on Christmas night trying to forge a plan for a future with a woman who clearly didn't want to have anything to do with me. For all I knew she patched things up with Dylan and they were back on track with her five-year plan.

No. She was done with him. She wouldn't do that. Would she?

I needed to get a grip on reality. If she wanted me to contact her she would've at least left her number. Damnit.

Maybe instead of strategizing about a life that involved Charlotte I needed to plan a future that didn't include her and come up with an idea on how to keep myself occupied until she was forgotten.

Distraction. I think that would work. I just needed to throw myself into my job and forget about her. It wasn't the first time a woman has walked out of my life and it wouldn't be the last.

TEN

CHARLOTTE

STARING at my empty closet in the apartment I shared with Dylan had my emotions running all over the place. I was closing a chapter in my life that I hadn't expected to ever end and that made me feel a little melancholy. I'd lived with Dylan for over a year and I'd thought he was the one with all my heart. I'd envisioned our wedding and porch swings with grandkids, the whole shebang. Realizing I'd been living with someone I didn't really know had been a hard pill to swallow. He wasn't the person I thought he was at all.

How was I so blind?

I closed my eyes and let out a few breaths just as a strong hand gripped the back of my neck and massaged gently. "Are you okay sweetie?"

"Yeah dad. I'm good." I was going to be just fine.

He held his hand out and helped me up. "The guys have you all loaded up. This is the last of it." He picked up the box I'd just packed.

We walked back out into the living room where his friends were all standing waiting for us.

"Thanks so much for helping me today I really appreciate it more than you know. I'm sure you all have much more interesting things you could be doing this New Year's Eve. If you want to come by the bar tonight drinks are on me." I gave them all a hug and we headed out. I took one last look at the apartment before I locked up.

By the time we got everything moved into storage and my parents place it was already three in the afternoon. I sat in my new bedroom thinking about what I'd lost but fantasizing about my new life and where things were headed.

This was a good thing.

I'd spent the last week thinking a lot about what happened and my goals and how I was going to achieve them. I'd thrown myself into my job taking on more hours than I could really handle but I wanted to move to Florida sooner rather than later so I needed to save as quickly as possible.

I tried extremely hard not to think about Ward and what he'd been up to. I figured that Mindy had moved back in and I just hoped things would be different this time around for them. I also hoped for their sake that he hadn't gone back to work twenty-four seven.

Ward had become someone special to me in the limited time we knew each other. And although my time with him was short it would always be a time in my life that I'd never forget.

I truly wished that we didn't live worlds apart because we could have been amazing friends. I was going to miss him so much but I'd promised myself I wouldn't dwell on it.

My reminder alarm went off on my phone telling me I needed to shower before work. Tonight would be an insanely busy shift seeing as it was New Year's Eve. I knew that most people wanted the Holidays off but not me. The tips were always awesome and the vibe was fun and exciting every time.

An hour later I walked into Drinks by Design with my New Year's Eve Crown on my head and went straight to my office. I had overlapped my schedule with Stacy tonight so I had some time for paperwork before I got behind the bar. After Jan quit last week I'd decided to take on more hours serving on top of my managerial duties which meant I'd been working sixty plus hours a week. Making drinks was a passion of mine though so it felt good to do it again instead of pushing paper day in and day out.

A knock at my office door broke me out of my

concentration. I looked up from the stacks of papers on my desk to see Stacy smiling grimly at me. "Sorry to interrupt Char but I was hoping you'd be able to come out onto the floor a little early tonight. We're slammed."

I looked over the paperwork in front of me. I'd made a large dent in them. "Give me ten and I'll be out."

"Yes!" She clapped her hands together. "Thank you." She turned and walked away leaving me to finish up what I could before helping out.

By the time Stacy left for the night I was regretting not scheduling more staff. I'd worked here for years and I'd never seen crowds like this. We'd had to start counting heads for fire code. I wasn't about to complain though. Spirits were high, the energy was infectious, and the tips were amazing. We had a great mix of clientele from lawyers to doctors to college kids and it just seemed to work well for us.

I'd been on my feet for five hours with two hours to go until midnight when Emily and Allison walked in. I hadn't seen them in weeks so I took my break to eat and catch up a little.

Emily and I had been friends since elementary school. We had the type of friendship that if we didn't speak all the time we never let that get in the way. We'd just fill each other in and go on like we'd just seen each other the day before. She'd started dating Allison just over a year ago and she was hilarious.

Allison set her menu down and sat back in her chair. "The sun kissed skin looks good on you Char. How was the trip?"

I thought about how to answer that question for a moment. "Well it was both the best and the worst vacation of my life."

Emily cocked a brow. "Do tell."

I ripped off the band aid and started with Dylan and his sexcapades before easing into Ward. I started off with every detail of our adventures and ended with how I completely embarrassed myself.

"Holy fuck!" Emily summed it up perfectly.

I shoved a fry in my mouth as Josh set down my plate. "I swear I couldn't make this shit up if I tried. Oh and I'm moving to Florida."

"What?" They said in unison.

I smiled back at them. "Yeah one thing I learned about myself by traveling to Malgaho Island is that I was meant to live by the sand and sea. I had never felt so at peace."

Emily stared at me for a moment. "You sure that wasn't *Ward*?" She waggled her brows suggestively.

"Yes. I'm positive." I was kind of sick of being asked that question. "Honestly the moment I stepped foot on the beach and looked out over the ocean I felt like I was home and for the record I hadn't even *met* Ward by this point."

Allison hummed. "Are you sure about this? It sounds to me more like you needed time away from real life. We all have that moment when we go away. It's energizing and feels great to have zero responsibility for the time being but it's not reality. You can move to the sunshine state but that won't get rid of the fact that you will still have a job and bills."

I thought about what she said but I knew deep down that wasn't it. "I get what you're saying but I don't think that's what it was. I guess I won't ever know until I try it. I've moved out of Dylan's place and I'm back home so I can save money quickly to move. I *need* to do this."

Emily's hand landed on Allison's on the table. "We'll support you either way but you better have a spare bedroom for us to come visit."

"Deal." I looked down at my phone. "I better get back to work. If I don't see you guys before then. Happy New Year." I hugged them both and headed back to the bar where I found Seth running around like crazy so I got back to work helping.

ELEVEN

WARD

"ARE YOU ALL RIGHT?" The lady sitting next to me smiled.

I regarded her for a moment. "Yeah. Why?"

She looked down at my hands and I followed her gaze. "You've been gripping your phone so tightly that your hands are turning white. You seemed to be fine for the last ten hours. Are you nervous about the plane landing?"

I eased up on my phone and let out an audible breath. "Not really. I'm more nervous about what awaits me when I land."

"Do you want to talk about it?" Her eyes crinkled in the corners as she smiled at me waiting for me to speak. "My name's Doris." She held out her hand for me to shake.

I took her hand hesitatingly. "Nice to meet you

Doris. I'm Ward." I wasn't really sure if I wanted to tell anyone anything but then I thought why not? I had nothing to lose. I took a deep breath and told her the entire story from start to end.

She listened intently and only spoke when I stopped. "Oh my. It seems like you've found the one haven't you?"

I chuckled. "I seemed to be oblivious to everything. I had my head stuck so far up my…butt that I couldn't see what was right in front of me. It wasn't until my brother—who is the last person I should be taking relationship advice from—shoved it all in my face. He made me see clearly and for that I will be forever grateful."

"So what's the plan?" She adjusted herself in her seat as if she were excited to hear it but she was going to be sorely disappointed.

I shrugged. "Honestly I don't have much of a plan. I know she lives in White Plains New York and that she works at a bar. That's the extent of it. I have no clue what I'll say when I find her or logistically how things will work out seeing that we live worlds apart but I am trying to think one step at a time."

"I think one step at a time is a good plan." She smiled softly at me. "You do have over an hour of thinking time though. So maybe come up with a speech of sorts."

She was probably right. "Thanks for listening."

She smiled and nodded before going back to her book.

My head fell back against the headrest and I closed my eyes. My mind raced with how things would go. I had no idea where she was or how I was actually going to find her but that wasn't going to stop me. It occurred to me that this process would've been a lot easier twenty years ago when we used phone books and everyone had a home phone. I'd scoured her social media and found no clue of where she was as it was locked down pretty tight. I had messaged her but I assume it's sitting in a request box nowhere to be found.

After some time of wracking my brain I finally gave up. I was just going to pour my heart out and tell her how I felt. Hopefully that would be enough.

I must have dozed off as the next thing I knew the pilot was telling us how cold it was on the ground and wishing us a Happy New Year.

My stomach knotted at the thought of finally seeing her. I looked down at my watch. It was already getting late. It was nearly ten thirty and we were only just disembarking.

If I wasn't so determined I would've checked into a hotel but I was really banking on finding her at work.

Stepping out of the airport into the frigid air was a

shock to my system. I'd bundled up in preparation but there was no way I could've been ready for this.

I pulled my collar up and hat down and hailed a taxi. I nearly threw myself into the back seat seeking the warmth I knew would be awaiting me inside.

The driver chuckled as I shivered in my seat. "Not from around here are ya?"

"What gave me away?" I snarled not meaning to sound as rude as I had. "Sorry. I'm honestly freezing. It was thirty degrees Celsius when I left home. What is it here? Zero?"

He hit a button on the dash. "You're pretty close. It's twenty-six which I believe is around minus five give or take. Where to?"

"White Plains." I couldn't elaborate much more than that.

He raised a brow in the rearview. "Address?"

"I don't have one. Just take me to a bar district if there is one and I'll find my way around." I couldn't for the life of me remember the name of the bar she worked at. "Hey. Do you know your way around White Plains? I'm looking for a bar that allows people to make their own drinks."

He hummed. "That does sound vaguely familiar. Let me think about it."

We drove in silence but by the time we pulled up to

a stop in front of what looked to be an office building I still hadn't figured out where I was going.

"I couldn't think of the name of the place you're looking for but this is the business district and therefor there are a lot of bars around here in either direction. Good luck finding it."

I swiped my card and thanked him with a hefty tip before stepping out into the freezing cold air.

I looked around having not a clue where to go. I decided to choose left and head in that direction. I read every sign I came across but nothing jogged my memory.

I'd been wandering around for almost an hour when it hit me. "Marlin!" I shouted scaring the crap out of a couple in front of me. *Why didn't I think of him before?*

It rang a few times before he finally picked up. "This better be important. I'm prepping for New Year's tonight and I'm way behind." He sounded out of breath.

My hand felt like it was going to fall off. "I'll make it quick. What's the name of the bar that Charlotte worked at?"

"Where are you?" He ignored my question.

I sighed. "New York. Wandering the streets. So what's it called?" I stopped on a street corner and waited for the light to turn.

"Wow. You're finally manning up? Good for you kid. It's called *Drinks by Design*."

That's it. "Thank you Marlin. You can go back to your preparations. I'm going to go find my girl." I hung up before he could say another word. I didn't want to hear a lecture on how it took me long enough. I mean it had only been a week.

I did a quick search on my phone for the bar and clicked on the map. I zoomed in and it looked like I was standing right on top of it. I looked around and scanned the names of the bars in the area then finally looked up. I was standing right in from of it. *Drinks by Designs* was lit up right above my head.

The door opened as someone walked in and I stood there frozen. I felt like I was going to be sick. Now that I was here I was having a panic attack.

"Are you coming in?"

I looked up to find a man smiling at me with the door open. I took a deep breath and stepped forward. "Thank you."

I walked inside and he followed behind taking off his jacket as he went. "Happy New Year, I'm Seth." He reached out.

I took his hand. "Ward. Happy New Year."

He smiled before walking away.

The room was packed with people dressed in jeans

and a hoodie to full on formalwear and they all seemed to be having a great time.

A voice came over the loudspeaker. "Thirty minutes until midnight."

I wandered around until I finally found the bar and noticed the same guy who let me in was behind it.

He nodded. "What can I get you?"

"Charlotte."

He smirked. "Hey man we all want a piece of that but she's taken."

My jaw hardened at the thought but I kept my cool. "Is she here?"

He looked me over as he contemplated how to respond. "Yeah she is. Can I tell her who's asking?"

My heart hammered in my throat as the realization that she was here hit home. I swallowed against the lump in my throat. "Yeah tell her—"

"Ward?"

I turned around to find Charlotte standing beside me with her mouth hanging open. She quickly recovered though. "What are you doing here?"

The tone of her voice had me pause. I wasn't sure if she was happy or not. All the words I'd said in my head over and over in the last twelve hours went out the window.

"I'm sorry. I would've called first but—" I didn't know what to say. "I didn't mean to intrude while you were at work. I just really wanted to see you and…" My words trailed off. I felt like a complete loser fumbling over my words while her co-worker watched.

A smiled crept up her face as she seemed to snap out of it. "It's completely fine. More than fine. Oh my God." She wrapped her arms around my neck. "How are you?"

I squeezed her tightly and took in her scent. *Home.* It was the first word that came to mind as I held her in my arms. I didn't want to let go but when Seth cleared his throat she pulled back.

I kept my hand on the small of her back though.

She looked over at Seth. "I should probably get back to work. I'm covering the other end of the bar if you want to try and find a space down there we can chat while I work."

I wanted to say no and demand we go somewhere I talk. Everything I needed to say to her was bubbling up inside me but I just smiled instead. "Lead the way." I turned and winked at Seth as we walked away. His friendly demeanor seemed to shift as he looked down at my hand on her back.

There wasn't a seat available so she grabbed me a stool from the back and placed me off to the side behind the bar instead.

She got to work making drinks as I looked on. I couldn't believe she was right there in front of me.

"So how have things been since you got home?" I figured small talk would be best at this point.

She nodded. "Good. I actually just moved back in with my parents seeing as I was homeless and all. I've thrown myself into work so I can save up to move to Florida."

"Oh wow. So you're actually doing it? Good for you." I was really proud of her. "Have you looked into where exactly?"

She shrugged. "A little but I haven't had much time. I think now that Dylan is behind me I will have a bit more time to do more research." She turned back to washing a beer mug in the sink. "So what brings you to New York?"

I wish I had something I could tell her either than the truth but I didn't. "You."

She whipped her head back. "Me? Why?"

I stood up and held her hands in mine. "Because I haven't been able to stop thinking about you ever since you left. You were still driving me crazy and you weren't even there."

She chuckled but I could see her eyes were welling up.

"I've had a week to think about things and with absolutely no way of contacting you I decided that I would come find you."

She looked up at me with wide eyes. "You flew all

the way here just to tell me I was driving you crazy from thousands of kilometers away?"

"That and—" I swallowed hard. "I want to be with you."

She blinked a few times. "You what?"

I reached up and swept her hair behind her ear. "I want us to be together. I know that things are complicated—"

"Complicated? You live in another country!" She tried to step back but I wrapped my arms around her waist.

I took a moment to compose myself. "I love you Charlotte. I've never felt anything like this in my entire life and it took you leaving to realize it. I should've asked you to stay but I knew that would be selfish of me. I know we live worlds apart but I will make this work even if I have to sit on a plane for twelve house every few weeks. I need you in my life."

A tear slipped down her cheek and I swiped it away with my thumb. "Please don't cry."

Her hands rested on my biceps and she looked down for a moment.

"Ten. Nine. Eight..." Everyone in the bar started counting down but neither of us joined in. I needed to know what she was thinking but I held my breath and waited.

"...One. Happy New Year!"

She looked up at me and then she stretched up and her lips touched mine. I was shocked but it took less than a second for me to reciprocate. He hands wrapped around my neck and I pulled her in close. Her mouth opened and our tongues danced as a version of Auld Lang Syne played in the background.

A few moments later she pulled back with a shy smile on her face. "As much as I would love to continue this…conversation, I have to get the champagne flowing."

"I can wait." And I did. When the bar finally closed at two I was still sitting there getting the death glare from Seth from across the room. I guess she hadn't told him that Dylan and she had broken up. Oh well. *You snooze you lose buddy.* I kept a friendly smile on my face because I wasn't going to let him ruin my mood.

She locked up and then looked up at me. "Where to?"

"Well seeing as that you live with your parents I think my hotel would be a better idea." I hoped she didn't take that the wrong way.

She kissed my lips. "Where are you staying?"

"Camstead Inn. Do you know it?"

She nodded. "This way." She took my hand and led me down the street.

It happened to be just around the corner. Thank God because I was freezing. We stepped through the front door of the beautiful large house and it was perfect. The architectural details throughout were stunning. It wasn't modern like Hale Court Inn, it was more of a classic look and with a shabby chic twist to it. A lot of weathered whites and greys with pops of limes and teal.

I checked in quickly and we made our way to my suite and opened the door hurriedly. The door clicked shut behind us and suddenly it was too quiet.

I looked around and spied a drink cart in the corner. "Would you like a drink?"

"Sure. Thank you." She walked over and sat on the sofa.

I set my bag down on the bed and made us both a rum and coke to make it easy and then took a seat beside her.

I lifted my glass. "Cheers to a new year and what might come."

She paused for a moment and then followed suit before clinking her glass with mine. "Cheers."

We both took a sip from our glasses and set them down on the coffee table.

I took a deep breath before turning toward her. "So now that we have a moment to talk. I know this is a lot to spring on you at once. I haven't a clue how this could work or even if you want to make a go at this. I guess I should ask that. What do you think?"

She was quiet for a second and my heart stopped but then she took my hand and smiled. "Honestly I've tried so hard to avoid any thoughts of you over the last week. I wasn't as successful as I would've liked.

"Umm...thanks. I'm only slightly insulted."

She smacked me playfully on the arm and giggled. "Shut up. You know what I mean."

"I do. I did the opposite though. I did nothing but think about you from the moment that you left. My family wouldn't get off my case and believe it or not it was my brother Dalton—the one who's never been in a relationship—who finally convinced me to come get you."

Her eyes went wide. "Come get me?"

I shook my head. "I didn't mean...I...I really don't know how we can make this work. I would never ask you to move to the island—"

"Why not?"

Now it was my turn for wide eyes. "Could I?"

"Didn't your mother ever teach you that it never hurts to ask?"

I was silent for a moment as I contemplated what she was saying. I hadn't even considered that as an option. "You're just messing with me aren't you?"

She burst out laughing.

"I knew it. You're such a brat.

"No." She shook her head and took a moment to

compose herself. "I was picturing how you'd be proposing to someone. Would you ask them if it was okay to pop the question?"

I felt like such an idiot. I had never been this nervous about anything in my entire life but I appreciated that she was trying to make light of it. I took a deep breath. "Listen. I've never felt like this about anyone before and I just need you in my life. Whether it's here in New York or down in Florida or on the island with me. I'll take you however I can get you."

The smile on her face was stunning. "Good save. I take back the proposal comment. I think you'd be great at it."

"Thank you..." My thoughts were all over the place and I had no clue where to start. "I just want to be with you." My words came out as more of a whisper.

She reached up and ran her hand across my jaw. she stared at me for a long moment and then her beautiful smile slowly returned. "Let's do this."

"Yeah? We can take things as slow as you need. I know you and Dylan just broke things off and you've made plans to move—"

Her finger touched my lips halting my ramblings.

"My plans were to move to the beach...wherever that may be."

My brow shot up and my heart picked up its pace.

"You mean...you would...really? You'd move to Malgaho Island? For me?"

"For us."

I couldn't believe she was willing to move. "I'm speechless."

"Good. Does that mean we're done talking? Because I'd really like to utilize that King size bed over there." She side eyed the bed and winked.

I was the luckiest guy on earth. This trip couldn't have gone any better in my dreams.

"You've made me the happiest guy ever." I stood up and lifted her off the sofa. Her legs wrapped around my waist and her lips found mine as I carried her to the bed.

I dropped her to the bed as she laughed.

I watched her from where I stood at the end of the bed with a smile. "God I love you." It was the second time I'd said it and it felt really good to tell her. Even if she wasn't quite there it was okay.

"Come here." She crooked her finger and I crawled on top of her. She took my face in the palm of her hands. "I love you too. I think I realized it on the last night of our getaway but I wasn't willing to admit it."

I chuckled. "You mean the night you were wasted and trying to sleep with me?"

"I was *not* drunk. I allowed you to think that because it made me feel better about you turning me down. I may have been tired and a little buzzed but I meant every word that I said that night and it crushed me that you didn't return my feelings."

I dropped my forehead to her and let out a loud breath. "Char." I shook my head. "I tried to talk to you that night. I was going to tell you how I felt but you blew me off. It took everything I had not to let things go further that night. I wanted you something fierce but not only did I think you were drunk but I knew you were leaving and I couldn't ask you to stay and leave your family behind."

"I'd gone to bed thinking that you wanted nothing to do with me since I was leaving. I mean what guy turns down a fling with no chance of commitment?"

I brought my lips to hers for a moment. "I knew that once I had you I wouldn't let you go and then I'd be some kind of asshole for asking you to give up your whole life for me."

She wrapped her arms around my neck. "How many times did you hear me talk about moving to the beach? Men can be so dense sometimes."

"Hey!" I did hear that but I figured Florida wasn't too far away from family. I let out a sigh. "Well I guess what's done is done. You're coming with me and I'm never letting you go. You better not get sick of the sun and beach like you did the winter because there's no turning back now."

She pulled my head down and brushed her lips lightly against mine. "You may regret this. I'm going to drive you crazy and won't allow you to be a workaholic."

A smirk crept across my face. "I'm well aware. I've finally found the woman that makes me not want to work twenty-four-seven. I never knew she was out there. Apparently she lived thousands of kilometers away in another country. I now believe in fate because there's no other explanation for you finding us in a magazine and three years later you're mine. It was divine intervention. I'll have to thank Dylan someday." I thought about that for a moment. "On second thought I'll send him a card. Not sure I want to speak with him."

"I guess things worked out for the best even if they didn't start off feeling that way."

EPILOGUE

CHARLOTTE

A YEAR AND A HALF LATER

"CHARLOTTE HONEY we're going to be late." My mom called from somewhere in the other room.

I laughed to myself. Only I would be late for my own event. "They can't start without me." I called back and I heard her grunt loudly.

Strong arms wrapped around my waist from behind and I felt his breath at my ear. "You're going to give your parents a panic attack on their first day of their vacation." He kissed slowly across my collarbone. "We really should get going."

I turned in Ward's arms and gripped the back of his neck. "I feel like I'm going to hurl."

"You're going to do amazing." He brought his lips

to mine and my anxiety waned. "Now get those sexy ass boots on and meet us out front."

Ward and I had eloped just six months ago. We had a beautiful Christmas themed reception a week later with fake snow and all. Today was the grand opening of his wedding gift to me.

He had given me a bar—well a shell of one and given me carte blanche to create whatever my heart desired. Tonight I was going to reveal my dream come true to everyone.

Ward hadn't even seen it yet.

I zipped up my thigh high black boots and did one last check in the mirror before heading out.

"What are you waiting for? Let's get going." I walked past them and my mom shot me a side-eye but didn't say a word as she followed behind me.

Everyone was quiet on the way over. Ward kept his hand on my thigh as he rubbed circles with his thumb while I stared out the window trying to breathe deeply over and over.

When we pulled up in front of the bar. I couldn't believe the turn out. The Hale family was well known and loved on the island and I'd been welcomed with open arms by the locals but this was much more than I could have ever hoped for.

I reached down and squeezed Ward's hand. "There are so many people here."

My mom's hand came up to rest on my shoulder from the back seat. "Are you ready?"

"Not really but I can't turn back now. Can I?"

We stepped out of the car and Ward tossed his keys to the valet as he rounded to my side. Everyone was clapping and cheering. I felt like a real celebrity.

My mom gripped my arm as I heard her sharp intake of breath telling me she'd noticed the name of the sign.

Laid-back Lily was a simple idea. Everyone was welcome and I wanted it to have a super relaxed vibe just like grandma Lily's house. She passed away just over a year ago so I thought it was the perfect way to honor her.

Although the bar was on the resort it was secluded and away from the main buildings which was perfect for people with prying eyes during the renovations. I couldn't wait for everyone to see what we'd done with the place.

We walked the red carpet and ducked under the ribbon that was tied across the entrance.

Ward handed me the microphone and whispered in my ear. "I love you and I couldn't be more proud of you."

I squeezed his hand as I took the mic and mustered up the courage to speak before I chickened out.

"Thank you so much for coming out tonight to celebrate the grand opening of Laid-back Lily. I hate public speaking so I'll be sure to make this quick. I want to thank my husband and his amazing family for their support throughout this process and allowing me to be a part of Hale Court Inn. I'd also like to thank my parents for putting up with me and keeping me from quitting countless times when things got tough. I hope you all enjoy Laid-back Lily and feel at home."

Everyone applauded and I cut the ribbon quickly.

Ward's hand rested on the small of my back as I pulled open the doors. Two of my new hostess staff grabbed the handles and held them open with a smile.

"Wow! Charlotte it's gorgeous." My mom's mouth hung open as she turned to look at me. "I'm so honored to be here with you for this. This is amazing." She pulled me in for a hug with her and my dad.

I held in the tears that were stinging the back of my throat. "Go. Look around. Grab a drink." I kissed them both on the forehead and shooed them off to enjoy the night.

Ward pulled me along to the back of the bar and stopped to look out over the ocean. The back wall opened up completely so it felt like the entire bar was on the beach. We had more seating outside than we did indoors.

"This is truly stunning Char. You've outdone yourself here." He pulled me into his arms.

I looked up at him and smiled. "You like?"

He shook his head and looked around again. "This is...I don't have any words for this. I'm not at all surprised though."

"Thank you. This was the best gift ever."

The noise in the bar started to increase as people started to fill the room. "I should probably get to work." I kissed his lips.

"Probably but remember our deal. No workaholics in this family."

I nodded. "Definitely not." We'd made a promise to each other before we left New York when we first got together that we'd never become workaholics again and that we'd make each other a priority and eventually when we had kids we would have lots of time to spend with them as well. "I love you."

"I love you too baby."

The night flew by and by the time the last person left it was almost three in the morning. It was just Ward and I sitting out on the back patio.

I held his hand in my lap. "I can't thank you enough. Since the moment you came into my life you've done nothing but make it better. I'm living a life I couldn't have even imagined and I have you to thank for that."

"Baby I'd give you the world because you've made mine." He kissed my forehead.

I looked around at and sighed contentedly. "I've never felt like I belonged anywhere but now with you I've found home both on the island and with you."

Don't miss out on news from

Kristie Leigh

Scan here to sign up

ACKNOWLEDGMENTS

I absolutely love the holidays including Christmas books and movies. I decided to write *Finding Home* pretty late in the year and I couldn't have done it without Shauna Casey. She was amazing and helped me from start to finish.

And of course I couldn't have done it without my bestie. She puts up with my incessant whining throughout each book. Through thick and thin this whore is always there for me.

With love and gratitude,

Kristie Leigh is a fiery redhead and USA Today Bestselling Author who fell in love with small-town life long before she ever experienced it. Growing up, she dreamed of quiet streets, friendly neighbors, and the kind of close-knit community that feels like home. Now, she's living that dream in a rural Alabama town with her high school sweetheart and their three kids.

Her passion for small-town romance comes alive in her stories, where back roads and burning hearts lead to love, second chances, and the kind of happily-ever-afters that stay with you long after the last page.

Discover more about

Kristie Leigh